Praise for *Pizza Girl*

'Jean Kyoung Frazier brings a flawless ear for language, great inventiveness, unfailing intelligence and empathy, and best of all a rare and shimmering wit. This novel has immense appeal'
Richard Ford

'Sharp and surprising, *Pizza Girl* shows us how obsession can fill the empty spaces in a young woman's life'
Julia Phillips, author of *Disappearing Earth*

'Sublime … irresistible and bold, brutal and sweet, with an ending that will thrash your heart'
Kimberly King Parsons, author of *Black Light*

'Luminous, brooding, and, frankly, awe-inspiring … Frazier has given us a gift'
Bryan Washington, author of *Lot*

'A sly, poignant glimpse into the wilds of suburbia, where intergenerational queer love and alienation from labor go hand in hand'
Andrea Lawlor, author of *Paul Takes the Form of a Mortal Girl*

'A funny and moving debut, full of wry observation and deep humanity'
Sam Lipsyte, author of *Hark*

'Darkly comic, unsentimental, subversive'
Elissa Schappell, author of *Blueprints for Building Better Girls*

Jean Kyoung Frazier lives in Los Angeles. *Pizza Girl* is her debut novel.

PIZZA GIRL

Jean Kyoung Frazier

ONE PLACE. MANY STORIES

This novel is entirely a work of fiction. The names, characters and incidents portrayed in it are the work of the author's imagination. Any resemblance to actual persons, living or dead, events or localities is entirely coincidental.

HQ
An imprint of HarperCollins*Publishers* Ltd
1 London Bridge Street
London SE1 9GF

This edition 2020

1
First published in Great Britain by
HQ, an imprint of HarperCollins*Publishers* Ltd 2020

Copyright © Jean Kyoung Frazier 2020

Jean Kyoung Frazier asserts the moral right to be
identified as the author of this work.
A catalogue record for this book is
available from the British Library.

ISBN: 978-0-00-835641-5

MIX
Paper from
responsible sources
FSC
www.fsc.org
FSC™ C007454

This book is produced from independently certified FSC™ paper
to ensure responsible forest management.

For more information visit: www.harpercollins.co.uk/green

Printed and bound by CPI Group (UK) Ltd, Croydon CR0 4YY

For my family, blood and chosen

PIZZA GIRL

1

HER NAME WAS JENNY HAUSER and every Wednesday I put pickles on her pizza.

The first time she called in it'd been mid-June, the summer of 2011. I'd been at Eddie's a little over a month. My uniform polo was green and orange and scratchy at the pits, people would loudly thank me and then tip me a dollar, at the end of shifts my hair reeked of garlic. Every hour I thought about quitting, but I was eighteen, didn't know how to do much of anything, eleven weeks pregnant.

At least it got me out of the house.

The morning she'd called, Mom hugged me four times, Billy five, all before I'd pulled on my socks and poured milk over my cereal. They hurled "I love yous" against my back as I fast-walked out the front door. Some days, I wanted to turn around and hug them back. On others, I wanted to punch them straight in the face, run away to Thailand, Hawaii, Myrtle Beach, somewhere with sun and ocean.

▼

I THANK GOD that Darryl's boyfriend fucked a Walgreens checkout girl.

If Darryl's boyfriend had been kind, loyal, kept his dick in his pants, I wouldn't have answered the phone that day. Darryl could make small talk with a tree, had a laugh that made shoulders relax—he manned the counter and answered the phones, I just waited for addresses and drove the warm boxes to their homes.

But Darryl's boyfriend was having a quarter-life crisis. Ketchup no longer tasted right, law school was starting to give him headaches, at night he lay awake next to the man he loved and counted sheep, 202, 203, 204, tried not to ask the question that had ruined his favorite condiment, spoiled his dreams, replaced sleep with sheep—is this it? One day, he walked into a Walgreens to buy a pack of gum and was greeted by a smile and a pair of D cups. The next day, Darryl spent most of his shift curbside, yelling into his phone. The front door was wide open, and I tried not to listen, but failed.

"On our first date you told me that even the word 'pussy' made you feel like you needed a shower."

It was the slowest part of the day. A quarter past three. Too late for lunch, too early for dinner, pizza was heavy for a mid-afternoon snack. The place was empty except for me and the three cooks. They waved hello and goodbye and not much else. I couldn't tell if they didn't speak English or if they just didn't want to speak to me.

"You know you've ruined Walgreens for me, right? I'm going to have to drive ten extra minutes now and go to the CVS to get my Twizzlers. God damn it, you know that I can't get through a day without my fucking Twizzlers."

I was sitting on an empty table, turning paper napkins into birds and stars and listening to my iPod at a volume that allowed me to think, but not too deeply. I couldn't remember the name of the boy I used to share Cheetos with in first grade. I wondered if I had ever used every drop of a pen's ink. All shades of blue made my chest warm.

Our boss, Peter, napped around this time. Every day, at 3:00 p.m. without fail, he'd close his office door and ask us to please, please not fuck anything up. We never fucked anything up. We also didn't get much done. I stared at a large puddle of orange soda on the floor and made a paper-napkin man to sit among the birds and the stars.

"Oh God, tell me you wore a condom."

The phone rang then. I was about to call for Darryl. He started shouting about abortion.

I'd be lying if I said I don't look back on this moment and feel its weight. I could've just let it ring—no one would've known. I didn't. I hopped off the table, walked to the counter, picked up the phone, and heard her voice for the first time.

"So—have you ever had the kind of week where every afternoon seems to last for hours?" Her voice was heavy, quivering, the sound of genuine desperation. Before I could reply, the woman kept talking. "Like, you'll water your plants, fold your laundry, make your kid a snack, vacuum the rug, read a couple articles, watch some TV, call your mom, wash your face, maybe do some ab exercises to get the blood pumping, and then you'll check the clock and thirteen minutes have passed. You know?"

I opened my mouth, but she kept on going.

"And it's only Wednesday! I'm insane, I know. I'm insane. But do you know what I mean?"

I waited a few beats to make sure she was done. Her breathing was loud and labored.

"Um, yeah," I said. "I guess."

"Yes! So—you'll help me?"

I frowned, started ripping up an old receipt. "I think you may have the wrong number."

"Is this Eddie's?"

"Oh, yeah. It is."

"Then this is exactly the right number. You're the only person who can help me."

I remember shivering, wanting to wrap this woman in a blanket and make her a hot chocolate, fuck up anyone that even looked at her funny. "Okay, what can I do?"

"I need a large pepperoni-and-pickles pizza or my son will not eat."

"I can put in an order for a large pepperoni pizza. We don't have pickles as a topping, though."

"I know you don't. Nowhere out here does," she said. "You're the sixth place I've called."

"So what are you asking?" I rubbed my lower back. It had been aching inexplicably the past couple of weeks. I figured it was the baby's fault.

"We just moved here a month ago from North Dakota.

My husband got an amazing job offer and we love it here, all the palm trees, but our son, Adam, hates Los Angeles. He misses home, his friends, he doesn't get along with his new baseball coach." She sighed.

She continued: "He's on a hunger strike. A couple days ago he came up to me and said, 'Mommy, I'm not eating a damn thing until we go back to Bismarck.' Can you believe that? Who has ever said that? Who likes Bismarck? And that potty mouth! Seven years old and already talking like a fucking sailor. How does that happen?"

I wasn't even sure if she was talking to me anymore. I looked at the clock and saw that I'd been on the phone for over five minutes. It was the longest conversation I'd had with someone other than Mom or Billy in weeks. Darryl too, I guess, but that felt like it didn't count.

"I'm sorry," I said, "I just still don't understand how I can help with this."

"There was this pizza place back home that used to make the best pepperoni-and-pickles pizza. I swear, I've tried doing it myself, just ordering a regular old pepperoni pizza and putting the pickles on after. He said it wasn't right, and when I asked him what wasn't right about it, he just kept saying, 'It's not right,' over and over, louder and louder, and wouldn't stop until I yelled over him, 'Okay, you're right! It's not right!'" She paused. "I just thought maybe if I could get him that pizza, something that reminded him of home, this silly hunger strike could end and he could start to love Los Angeles."

There was a long pause. I would've thought she'd hung up if not for that loud, labored breathing.

When she spoke again, her voice was softer. I thought of birds with broken wings, glass vases so beautiful and fragile I was afraid to look at them for too long. "It just feels like I've been failing a lot lately," she said. "I can't even get dinner right."

I thought of a night two years ago. Dad was still alive and living with us. The Bears game had just started. He wasn't drunk yet, but by halftime he'd have finished at least a six-pack. Some nights, I was the best thing that ever happened to him, his pride, his joy; he talked often of buying us plane tickets to New York City and taking me to the top of the Empire State Building. On other nights, I was a dumb bitch, a waste of space; sometimes he'd throw his empties at me. I didn't want to find out what type of night it was. My window opened out onto the roof. I climbed out of it to sit and smoke, try to find stars in the sky. I was about to light up when I looked down and saw Mom's car pull into the driveway.

I watched as she took the key from the ignition, killed the lights. I waited for her to come inside. She didn't. She sat in the driver's seat, just sat. Five minutes went by and she was still sitting, staring out the windshield. I wondered what she was staring at, if she actually was staring at anything, or if she was just thinking, or maybe trying not to think, just having a moment when nothing moved or mattered—I wished that she was at least listening to music. She sat and stared another ten minutes before going inside.

There was a supermarket not far from Eddie's. Pickles were cheap. "What's your address?" I asked.

▲

THE COOKS EYED ME FUNNY when I came into the kitchen with a brown paper bag. They looked only slightly less nervous when I pulled a pickle jar out of it.

"It's okay," I said. "I'm just helping this lady out."

They stared blankly at me.

"Her kid isn't eating."

Silence.

"Can you guys get me a large pepperoni?"

They looked at each other, shrugged, and started pulling the dough. I chopped a couple pickles into uneven slices and wedged myself between the cooks, sprinkled the pickles over the sauce, cheese, and meat. I told myself that it only looked off because it was raw, but the cooks didn't seem to know what to make of it either. One sniffed it, another laughed, the third just stared and scratched his head. They eventually shrugged again and put the pizza in the oven.

While I waited, I walked out of the kitchen and to the front of the shop. Darryl was off the phone and back inside, pouring rum into a soda cup. We stared at each other for a moment. His eyes were red and puffy; his face looked strange without a smile.

I coughed, just for something to do. "Any calls?"

"Just one," he said. "Midway through, the guy decided he wanted Chinese and hung up."

"Cool. I picked up one while you were—when you—" I coughed again. "Cool."

I thought about asking him if he was okay, decided to

mop the floor instead. Peter would be waking up soon and didn't need much to start yelling at us. Darryl sipped his drink and wiped down the counter.

I mopped half the shop before my mind began to wander. There was a slip of paper in the back left pocket of my jeans with an address and the name Jenny Hauser scribbled above it.

"I'm Jenny, by the way. Jenny Hauser," she'd said after she thanked me for the third time. "My grandma also had the same name. I don't remember much about her except that she made real good rhubarb pie and hated black people."

I'd thought she sounded too old to be a Jenny. She should be a Jen or a firm Jennifer—Jenny had a ponytail and scrapes on her knees, liked the crusts cut off of her PB and J's, fought with her mom but always apologized, had never really been in love but had plenty of crushes on boys in her class, teachers who showed her kindness, Jenny believed in God and Kenny Chesney—I couldn't stop imagining what she looked like.

"Yo," Darryl hollered. "Order up."

MY DAD DIDN'T HAVE ANY MONEY to leave us. He did have a '99 Ford Festiva.

The paint job was faded, the driver's door dented; there was a questionable yellow stain on the back seat; the A/C was broken, stuck on high, freezing air pumped through the car, even in the winter. Simply put, the car was a piece of shit.

I'd told Mom we should sell it for parts, take whatever

we could get. She shook her head and said she couldn't, she remembered him bringing it home for the first time. "He looked so handsome stepping out of it. He bought me flowers too," she said. "Sunflowers." I didn't remember that. I did remember him teaching me to drive in it. He'd smoke and sip from his red thermos, flick ashes on me whenever I drove too slow or forgot to signal. Once, I sideswiped a car in a Popeyes parking lot and he made me iron his shirts and shine his shoes every Sunday night for a month.

When Mom got a new car last year—a used '07 Toyota Camry that didn't have dents or stains or broken radios, was a sleek shiny silver—she dropped the keys to the Festiva on my bedside table. I let the car sit in front of the house a week before I lost all willpower.

I spent that whole day driving, every song sounded good on full blast. It was a Los Angeles winter day, seventy and cloudless. Everything looked crisp and clean through the windshield. The full gas tank and the open road made my fingers and toes tingle. A man was selling oranges on the shoulder of a highway. I bought four bags and shouted along with a song that was about a girl and a goat and Missoula, Montana.

THE RADIO WAS OFF when I was driving to Jenny's house for the first time. My palms were sweaty against the steering wheel and I had that tight-chest feeling I sometimes got when I drank too much coffee. I hadn't had any coffee for over a week. Billy said it was bad for the baby, he didn't want to have a little girl or boy with twelve toes and poor reading skills.

The address took me to a nice part of town where all the homes were big and uniform with perfectly mowed front lawns. I saw three different golden retrievers being walked by three different women in tracksuits before I pulled up to her home. I was relieved to see that, though her home was big, it didn't annoy me. It was one of the smaller ones on the block, and her lawn was slightly overgrown and yellowing in some places.

The coffee chest–feeling increased as I stepped out of my car and started walking to the front door. I appreciated then how good I felt on a daily basis, calm and centered, how little fazed me, my ability to walk tall and look straight ahead. Three weeks ago I peed on a stick, and when the little pink plus winked up at me, I walked downstairs, opened the freezer, and ate a Popsicle, thought about what I wanted to watch that night, a rom-com or an action movie—both would have broad-chested dudes, did I want to cry or see shit get blown up?

There was sweat in places I didn't know I could sweat. I was confused why this instance of all instances was making me damp behind the knees, between my toes. As I knocked on Jenny's door, three times hard, I reminded myself that she was just some lady with some kid. Then she opened the door and I wanted to take her hand and invite her to come with me whenever I ran away to Myrtle Beach.

2

I'D LIVED in the same house my whole life. It was small, in a neighborhood with some crime, rarely bad crime. Only four or five people a year got stabbed, a shooting here and there, rarely fatal. The worst that usually happened was some chubby boy getting kicked in the ribs and mugged, a rock thrown through a window, bikes swiped off the front lawn, walls tagged, sidewalks crowded with empty cans and chip bags, whatever shit happened when people were drunk, or high, or bored, or all three.

Dad had often been heard arguing with people who said the neighborhood was shit. He'd often repeat himself:

"It's called Character Building. If I didn't get knocked around every now and then, I wouldn't be who I am today."

"It's called Natural Selection. If you're dumb enough to leave your shit out, it should be stolen."

"It's called Being Proactive. If you don't like trash, bend down and pick it up."

"It's called Shutting the Fuck Up. If you don't like it, move somewhere else."

I'd never hop onto his side of an argument, holler and spit in people's faces, but I didn't mind where we lived either.

BACK AT HOME, Billy had a surprise waiting for me in bed.

"Where the fuck did you get a cat?"

A fat orange tabby lay on my pillow, licking itself. His eyes were large and green and watched my every move. I went to the other side of the room to hang up my coat, and his eyes followed me the entire time. I immediately knew we were not going to get along.

"Super-cute, right?" Billy flopped on the bed and started rubbing the cat's belly. He stretched and purred and, I swear, he smiled. "I feel like if he was a human he'd be chubby and his clothes would be stylish, redneck chic. A NASCAR dad that also reads The New Yorker. A lover, not a fighter."

The cat's purring grew louder and I wasn't surprised—four legs, two legs, whatever, you'd have to be crazy not to love Billy Bradley.

When I first brought him home to meet Mom, he took his shoes off at the front door and ate every scrap off his plate, told Mom it was the best meal he'd had in a while, maybe ever. As he got up to go to the bathroom, she whispered loudly in my ear, "Hold on to this one." He finished two more helpings and, before he left, kissed me on the cheek, and gave Mom a good long hug, told her he'd definitely be back. The second the front door clicked behind him, Mom was gushing. "Lovely! An absolutely lovely boy!" She adored everything about him, especially his Americanness. His very name made her want to sing "The Star-Spangled Banner." A year later, when I told Mom that I was pregnant, she cried tears of joy—her daughter would get to stay under her roof and she'd have an American husband and a true American baby.

"The Halperns' little girl found him next to a dumpster behind the 7-Eleven. She wanted to keep him. Her parents wouldn't let her, said he could have fleas." Billy worked for his uncle's landscaping company. They had a couple city contracts, but made most of their money mowing large lawns in rich neighborhoods.

"Lucky us."

Billy frowned, sat up quickly. "Wait, are you mad? Please don't be mad."

"I'm not mad," I said. "I just—"

"Look, you won't even have to do any of the hard stuff." He grabbed my wrists and kissed the back of my hands. "I'll feed him, water him, change his litter box, you can just pet him and love him, read to him, maybe. I bet he would love it if you just sat with him in your lap and read from your books. I thought it could be a nice way to get ready. Plus, you know Billy Jr. is going to love having a furry friend around."

He wrapped his arms around my waist, buried his face in my neck, pressed more kisses there. "Please don't be mad."

It took me a second, but I hugged him back.

"I'm not mad." I kissed him once, on the cheek, pulled

away, and looked at the cat. "I guess he is kind of cute. Does he have a name?"

"We'll come up with something. We can ask Mom." He pulled me back into his arms. "Why don't you shower and change and come downstairs for dinner when you're comfortable?"

One more kiss and he was out the door. I reached over to pet the cat and he hissed at me, ears flattened and eyes wild.

BILLY AND I wouldn't have met if his parents hadn't celebrated their twentieth anniversary in Costa Rica.

I was a junior with a bad haircut who ditched classes to smoke weed and nap in my car, had a few friends out of social necessity, sat quietly at corner tables in the cafeteria and read, repeating platitudes in my head like "Life is only just beginning," trying to make them ring true. Billy was an honors student, the captain of the baseball team and the Mathletes, sat at a table in the center of the cafeteria and entertained his overpacked table—his laugh could be heard even once I'd dumped my tray and went outside.

But Billy's mom wanted to go zip-lining and see a real live toucan, lie nude on beaches and drink colorful fruity drinks. Billy's dad wanted what Billy's mom wanted.

The trip was perfect until, on their last night, it began pouring rain and a sheep escaped from its pen. Excited by its newfound freedom, it ran into the street where Billy's parents were driving, doing their best to imprint every detail of the Costa Rican landscape into their minds. Billy's dad was a veterinarian; he swerved hard to avoid hitting the sheep, and their car spun on the slick road and off a cliff. The doctors said they both died instantly, painlessly.

Dad had died a week earlier. Soon, Billy was sitting across from me in a circle of other people who were dealing with Grief and Loss of a Loved One. The meetings were held in the local church every Wednesday at 5:00 p.m. The cookies were stale. Fortunately, the coffee was strong. We sat and listened as people wept and worried that they'd never be the same. Billy and I were the only two who never cried, although he did look sad, different, unlike the large, laughing boy whose warm presence I'd taken for granted.

One day after the meeting, he asked me if I liked ice cream. I said not really, but that I would go with him.

We sat in silence as he ate three separate cones. I was about to tell him that he could've saved money and just gotten a triple scoop when he blurted out that he felt bad that he didn't feel more bad.

"Things really haven't been so different since they died," he said, looking down at his empty, sticky hands. "I didn't see them much. They always seemed to love each other more than me, were always going on romantic dates or taking trips together. I kind of felt like their third wheel, an afterthought. The house has always been quiet." He looked at me then, only for a second. "I just see all those people in there sobbing and I'm so damn jealous." He chewed on his lip, began shredding the napkin in front of him, and I felt something in me twist and soften—I had the same nervous habit. "Sorry," he said. "That was fucked up."

I noticed his shoulders then, how strong they looked,

like they were made of beef and steel. I pictured trees, mountains, boulders, birds' nests, all of the Los Angeles skyline resting upon them.

I grabbed both of his hands in mine, tight. "Do you want to come back to my place?"

I LOCKED THE CAT in my room and went downstairs. Mom was knitting tiny sweaters in neutral colors while Billy was in the kitchen making *pajeon* shaped like barn-yard animals. For the past couple weeks, Mom had been teaching Billy how to make basic Korean dishes: "The baby can have your hair. He's going to have our taste buds."

Mom came to the United States after her mom's brother wrote to her that he'd found the promised land: Champaign-Urbana, Illinois. He owned a convenience store and could always use more help. After months of paperwork and waiting in long lines, Mom and her family were on a fourteen-hour flight straight to Chicago.

She was seventeen when they got there—young enough to be molded, not so young that she hadn't already begun to want certain things, big things. She worked long hours at the convenience store, and when it was slow, studied English, determined to lose her accent, dreamed of the University of Illinois. All the UI students who came in to buy candy, cigarettes, condoms, and booze seemed so attractive and happy. She became obsessed with Ameri-canness, wanted nothing more than to be a part of the red, the white, the blue.

One of the university students came in every morning

to buy a pack of Luckies and two forties. He was tall and broad and 100 percent American, always smiled at her, asked her how her day was going, remembered her name, said it with a soft Midwestern twang as he walked out of the store. At night, he'd come back, buy two more forties, and wait until closing. They'd sit on the bus bench outside, talking for hours, passing the bottle back and forth, even though Mom hated beer.

Two months later, they were moving to Los Angeles. He wanted to write movies and make millions. She wanted him and to wake up every morning, look out her window, see the Pacific Ocean. Eleven months later, I was born.

I stopped on the edge of the staircase and stared at Mom as she knitted and thought about how our house was thirty minutes from the beach.

She looked up and noticed me, smiled wide. "How are my babies doing?" Billy turned around and smiled too. They stopped what they were doing and got up to hug me. They formed a warm, loving wall around me, rubbed my belly, and whispered to it. I couldn't hear what they were saying.

We sat down and they started talking about what they always talked about.

First, they asked how I was feeling, and after I gave my usual "Fine, good. Yeah, I'm good," they launched into more important subjects—what gender the baby would be (they both were sure it was going to be a boy), strong manly names (John, Matthew, Jacob, other Bible men, even though we weren't religious), color of the nursery (a classic blue or a bold red), potential godfathers and godmothers (lots of names of family members I didn't know), should we already start saving for private school (absolutely, yes), etc.

I nodded and smiled, said "uh-huh" at the right times. I was feeling fine until Mom brought up the name "Adam," perfect for a first child.

My face stayed normal and I managed to eat more than half my plate, but I was gone, done for; my mind was on Jenny Hauser's ponytail.

HER PONYTAIL was the longest I'd ever seen on a woman her age.

Most moms in my neighborhood kept their hair short or bobbed, muted, as if to have physical proof of their seriousness, their superior mothering ability—my thank-you card is nicer than your thank-you card, don't you dare try and sign up for more Neighborhood Watch shifts than me, this marijuana is medicinal. Jenny's hair spilled down her back, didn't stop until it was hovering just above her butt.

She had to be at least forty, probably closer to forty-five. Her body looked soft, once fit. Her jeans were baggy and shapeless and there was a stain on the collar of her shirt. I hoped that the stain was new. It seemed more likely that she'd been wearing the same shirt for several days. There were lines around her eyes and mouth, two deeper ones on her forehead. I wanted to touch them with my fingertips, smooth them out. When she spoke, her voice cracked on the first word, like she hadn't said anything out loud in a while.

"Jesus Christ," she'd said. "Your uniforms are truly terrible."

"I know."

"Green and orange. Like Kermit the Frog fucked a pumpkin."

"The Hulk ate a bunch of Doritos and took a shit."

She laughed and her eyes got squinty, crinkled at the edges. I didn't want to smooth out all her lines. "Truly, though, thank you for this," she said. "I can't believe you actually came."

The air turned thick and I found it impossible to look her in the eye. I wanted to be wearing a big jacket and a hat I could pull down low. I mumbled, "No problem," and handed her the pizza.

I was about to turn and sprint back to my car when she said, "Oh! I have to pay you!" She slapped her forehead. "And tip you! I absolutely have to tip you. Hold on, my wallet is lying around somewhere."

She disappeared into her house and I stood there awkwardly, shifting my weight from foot to foot. I planned on politely waiting there, staying outside, but the door hung wide open and something caught my eye.

The home's entrance was pristine, a word I'd never used to describe anything before. An intricate Persian rug, shoes lined up evenly on both sides, a center table topped with a vase of real flowers, fancy flowers, not corner-market $9.99-for-a-dozen roses, all of this underneath a crystal chandelier—none of this was what interested me.

The front of the house may have been pristine, but just beyond, into the living room, it was chaos.

There could've been another beautiful rug, there could've just been carpet, it was impossible to tell. Clothes covered every inch of the floor. On the couch there was an empty bag of Hot Cheetos, a half-eaten salad, a tub of cream cheese. The table was crowded with magazines and paper plates covered in various pools of paint. Seven chairs looked like they'd been brought in from the dining room and were serving as easels for her paintings.

I had never been alone in someone else's house. Slow steps forward, a pause after each, a moment to consider the wrongness of what I was doing—how rude of me to violate her private space with my eyes, to let the bottoms of my shoes sink into her carpet and leave behind the filth of where I'd been, she would be back at any moment, what would I say then? The next minute I'd see something new that would wipe the guilt from my thoughts and leave behind only curiosity, bright and shiny and begging to be stroked—I couldn't stop thinking about how, at one point or another, everything in the room had been touched by her hands. I walked through Jenny's living room turning my head left and right, fists clenched at my sides.

I went to the nearest chair and inspected its painting closely—it was terrible. They were all terrible. Two were rudimentary portraits of turtles, two were blocky houses in open fields, one was full of unintelligible blobs, one was just three different shades of blue, the last was blank, still lovely with possibility.

"Yikes. Hi."

I turned around to see Jenny standing behind me, a twenty in hand, and a look I couldn't read on her face. We stood facing each other in silence among the clutter and paintings. All the apologies I could think of sounded more like pleas—I'm sorry, please, I do things without thinking and I don't know how to stop. Before I could say anything, she surprised me again by laughing. "So—I guess now you really think I'm crazy."

She cleared her throat. "So let me explain."

She pointed to the floor. "Old T-shirts to catch any paint that I spill."

She pointed to the couch. "I actually attempted a healthy lunch, but my mouth got bored. Have you ever tried dipping your Hot Cheetos in cream cheese? What? No? Do it. One-hundred-Michelin-star rating." She paused. "Now, the paintings. What do you think?"

"Oh. Well."

She laughed again and I found myself becoming used to the sound. "It's okay," she said. "You don't have to worry. This isn't a hobby of mine. I have no secret burning desire to become a painter. I was just in my son Adam's room earlier and I realized he had no decorations on his walls and I thought I'd try and make some for him, brighten the space a little. As you can see, I forgot a very important detail." She spread her arms wide. "I suck at art."

"I like that one turtle," I said. "His head is weird and dented. Like he got hit with something hard."

"Yeah? Thanks. Turtles are Adam's favorite animal. He wants to go to Hawaii so he can swim with them."

I checked my watch; I'd been gone for way too long. I was about to ask for the money when I felt my lunch rising in me—a slice of pizza and a Snickers bars—ran toward a closed door that looked like it would lead to a bathroom, but was actually to a closet. I sunk down to my knees, grabbed the least expensive-looking thing, a rain boot, and puked in it.

The puke was watery—I could see a full, undigested circle of pepperoni—I puked some more and felt a hand on my shoulder, turned around to see Jenny hovering behind me. "I'm sorry," I said, "I—"

"You're pregnant." She helped me off the ground, her smile stretched and warm, and I wished that a detail other than my pregnancy had made her look that way. "Congratulations! You doing this favor for me is proof you're going to be a great mom."

I almost puked more, but swallowed it down.

I didn't know if I was noticeably showing yet and I was doing my best not to find out. In the mornings, before I showered, I'd undress with my back to the mirror. When I walked, I'd keep my head up and eyes focused straight ahead, I avoided looking down. It made my palms itch to think about the day when I wouldn't be able to fit into any of my clothes.

My hands went to my belly as if to cover it. "Thanks."

She frowned. "You're not excited." It wasn't a question. She said it firmly, unblinking, a statement.

I lied often. It was just simpler that way. As a little kid, I remember being told repeatedly that lying was bad, lying never fixed anything, Abraham Lincoln freed the slaves and never lied. But no one ever told me how wonderful and easy it was to lie, how many conversations it would save me from and the stares it would avert—"Yeah, I'm

fine!" "What? No, I'm not mad!" "Don't worry, it's okay!"—
and did Abraham Lincoln really never, ever lie? In bed
at night during the Civil War, did he toss and turn and
soak his sheets with sweat and eventually wake Mary Todd
to tell her, "Hold me, I'm scared, I think I fucked up," or
did he lie awake and sweat quietly, working his hardest
to remain still, to keep his mouth shut, to let Mary Todd
sleep soundly and unaware?

Lying was simpler. I repeated this in my head over and
over as I stood in Jenny's living room looking at everything except her—each shitty painting, the blank canvas,
the tub of cream cheese, the old T-shirts on the ground.
I kept returning to one T-shirt. It was purple and had a
large cobra head in the center with the words "Excellence
is" underneath. The rest of the sentence was cut off by a
Hawaiian shirt.

"Hey, you okay?"

I looked away from the cobra and back to Jenny. She was
staring at me with wide eyes, her mouth hanging open a
little. I noticed a piece of lettuce stuck between her bottom front teeth and I desperately wanted to reach over
and pull it out, let my fingers linger in her mouth and spit,
and I knew I wouldn't be able to lie, even if it was easier.

"No," I said. "I'm not excited."

She looked away from me and I regretted saying anything, regretted that I spoke truth and it revealed my ugli-
ness, let it breathe and writhe in the daylight. Then she
looked back at me and said, "Good."

"What?"

"It's good you're not excited. Or it's good you know

you're not excited." Her voice was different now, more like it was when I first heard it on the phone—low, trembling, a voice standing on the top of a ladder, the lip of a skyscraper, the peak of a mountain, a voice that can't help but look over the edge even though it knows this will serve only as a reminder that it's a long way down, a voice that needed to be cradled, tucked in gently each night. "People will always love telling you how you're supposed to be feeling and it will always make you feel *less than* when you don't feel it. I'm sorry if I was being one of those people." She shook her head. "How old are you?"

"Eighteen."

"I'll tell you what I wish someone told me when I was eighteen—it never goes away."

"What is 'it,' exactly?"

"All of it, any of it, just it." Suddenly, she reached out and pushed a loose strand of my hair behind my ear. "Jesus, you're so young. Of course you're not excited."

She kept staring at me and I was worried that she was going to ask more, that I would dump the weight of my life among her living-room clutter. She just turned, grabbed the turtle painting, and handed it to me. "For the baby. Boy or girl, everyone likes turtles."

I wasn't much of a crier—Billy and I had rented *Toy Story 2* last week and the collar of his shirt was damp by the end, mine dry. As I took that shitty painting I felt weirdly close to tears.

"Here's money for the pizza, keep the change." She handed me a twenty and pulled out another, pressed it firmly into my palm. "And a little extra for you, my savior."

She walked me to the front door and hugged me and I didn't mind. She smiled and I wanted to bottle it up, pour it over my morning cereal. "Take care, Pizza Girl."

The door shut and I stared at it, tried to come up with reasons to knock and bring her back.

IT WAS A BLESSING I didn't get into a car accident. I spent the rest of my shift in a daze. My hands and feet felt and behaved like bricks. I knocked over a stack of boxes and dropped a napkin dispenser I was trying to refill. As Darryl bent down to help me clean up, he asked me if I'd taken pulls from his Bacardi.

I mixed up orders. Drew Herold got Patty Johnston's Meat Lovers, extra bacon. Patty Johnston got Drew Herold's Very Veggie, no sauce. "You might as well just get a salad," she said, shaking her head, inspecting a mushroom between her fingers. She was nice, an older mom type who looked like she was used to dealing with youthful incompetence. She didn't mind having to wait while I drove back to retrieve her pizza, just told me to include garlic bread sticks for free next time she called in. Drew Herold was less nice, told me that meat was murder, he'd be calling Domino's in the future.

When I got back to the shop, I went to the bathroom and didn't notice the seat was up. There was toilet water on my pants as Peter yelled at me. Driving home, I missed the turn for my street three times. I kept getting distracted by lamppost lights—I saw Jenny standing underneath each one. She was still lovely, even under their harsh orange glow.

▼

AT NIGHT, after Billy was snoring in my ear and I heard Mom flick off the TV and double-lock the front door, I'd run my hands through Billy's hair twice and then quietly get out of bed. I'd tiptoe down the stairs and into the backyard, walk across the lawn, and go inside Dad's shed.

In his last years, Dad spent most of his time in here. When he got home from whatever his current job was, when Mom or I pissed him off, when he just needed a breath, some "Me Time," he'd throw open the screen door and stomp across the lawn, lock himself in the shed for hours.

The shed was always padlocked. He repeated over and over that Mom and I were forbidden to go inside. A little after he died, I got a hammer and swung at the lock until it broke off.

I didn't know what to expect, but I realized then a part of me hoped that whenever he went into the shed he'd feel bad about what he'd said, how he acted, his boozy, sour breath. He'd feel bad and he'd grab his toolbox or notebook and try to make us something to apologize, would write long letters to us promising to be a better man. I pictured him whittling little sculptures, painting them bright, hopeful colors. His letters would contain beautiful, flowery language.

When I went inside there were no tools, or papers, or paints. There was just an old armchair, a small TV on a table barely big enough to support it, a mini-fridge. Empty beer cans and cigarette butts covered most of the floor. There were a pile of old newspapers and a foam football in the corner.

I thought about going back into the house and getting a book of matches, watching the shed burn before my eyes. I didn't. I sat in the armchair and cried for the first and only time since he died.

Ever since Billy and I decided we'd be keeping the baby, I'd been coming to the shed most nights. I'd sit in the armchair and flick on the TV to the infomercial channel— there was something weirdly peaceful about people enthusiastically trying to sell you things. After a while, I'd open the fridge and pull out a beer. It was lite beer, I reasoned, basically water. I would only have one, sometimes two if the day had been long and my head and body both felt heavy. I'd drink slowly, try and empty my mind, focus on the infomercials and how much better my life could be if I had a Snuggie, or a Shake Weight, or Ginsu Steak Knives— I'd be warm, fit, and able to slice through anything.

It was the best part of my days.

I was halfway through my third beer when I remembered. I walked out of the shed and to the front of the house and unlocked the trunk of my car, grabbed Jenny's painting.

There were no nails to hang it, so I just leaned the misshapen turtle against the wall with the TV. It looked good there.

3

"AT TWELVE WEEKS, the baby is the size of a plum."

The clinic doctor told me this with a smile as he squirted gel onto my belly. The gel was a translucent blue, felt slimy and cold. Alien spit, I thought.

"Like what type of plum? And how ripe is it?" I shivered as I watched him spread the gel around. "At the supermarket, plums come in lots of different sizes."

The doctor standing above me was an old man with hair coming out of his nose and ears. His hands looked older than the rest of him—large and gnarled, veins popping out, deeply lined palms—I wondered when the last time he had sex was, what those hands felt like against bare thighs. His name tag literally read Dr. Oldman and I would've laughed if I hadn't been lying on my back, shirt up, sweaty and alone. I couldn't stop imagining a plum in my stomach.

"You're a funny girl," he said.

I imagined the plum growing arms and legs and trying

to communicate with me. I couldn't or wouldn't understand. The plum quickly gave up on me and started banging its tiny fists against the inner walls of my stomach, dug
its teeth into me, and drew blood. I shivered again.

The night before, Billy had rubbed my shoulders and
offered to come with me, but the appointment was at
nine. Landscaping crews did their biggest jobs before
the sun reached its full power—a few parks, schools, one
cemetery—since hard work was a little less hard when
sweat wasn't pouring into your eyes, the back of your
neck wasn't red and burnt, thirstiness was a feeling that
started in your throat and spread to your mind. I kissed
both of Billy's eyelids and told him that I would be fine, he
shouldn't skip work, we couldn't afford that.

The money Billy's parents left him had been huge in
helping us with bills, groceries, a fun trip to the movies
here and there, and we both tried not to think about how
the total was deflating at a rapid rate. Mom was a checker
at Kmart and the job sucked—she'd been working there
for ten years and had only just received her first raise, a
dollar more per hour—but we were lucky they provided
insurance. I held Billy's large, sweet head between my
hands and told him to go to work, I'd be fine, would make
sure to bring home the first picture of Billy Jr.

As I lay there watching Dr. Oldman set up the ultrasound
equipment, I tuned out his small talk about his daughters—
there were five of them, all named after famous mountain
ranges—and forced myself to wonder why I really didn't
want Billy to come with me to the appointment.

Yes, it was true that there was a never-ending list of

things Billy and I needed and that most of those things were tied to money. At night we'd strip naked and cuddle in bed, taking turns being big spoon, and going on and on about how dope life would be if we had a bottomless bank account.

No question, we'd quit our jobs. Mom had been good to us, we'd buy her her own place, one with a front- and backyard, a kitchen worthy of her skill, finally by the ocean, close enough that if she opened the windows sand would get blown in by the sea breeze. With Mom taken care of and our schedules open, next we'd buy a new car, something fast and flashy and gas-inefficient, red or yellow, maybe a sharp electric blue, good-fucking-bye to that goddamn Festiva. Billy had a book of U.S. maps. We'd pore over the pages and debate where to drive first, where we wanted the baby to be born—"How cool would it be to say you were from Zzyzx, California?" We'd go back and forth for a while until Billy would shrug and smile. "Let's just go everywhere, literally every city in America. I want to go everywhere with you. The baby will be cool no matter where he's from."

This was all talk, though, something to occupy our minds and fill our sleep with big, bright images. Billy was content with our life, what we had was more than enough for him, and I was pretty sure it was enough for me too. We would find ways to make money and get by. He could've definitely skipped work to come with me to our baby's twelve-week ultrasound.

In the week leading up to the appointment, every time

I pictured Billy standing by my side and holding my hand, sweat would begin to collect on my upper lip. Mom always told me that this was how she knew when I was nervous, Dad used to nervous-sweat too. She remembered on their wedding day standing at the altar before him, hoping that he'd wipe his lip with the back of his hand before he kissed her.

Even just picturing Billy next to me at that moment in the clinic, I could feel the lip sweat forming. He would've been his lovely, charming self, making small talk right back with Dr. Oldman, asking polite questions while also being funny—"What're your daughters' names? I can only guess one: Sierra Nevada. You didn't name one Kiliman-jaro, did you?" Their joint laughter echoed in my head, and I felt the pits of my shirt begin to grow dark and wet.

Dr. Oldman must've noticed the sweat. "Hey, now, there's no reason to be scared." He patted my shoulder warmly. "This is a happy day. Let's go take a closer view of this baby."

He pressed the transducer against my belly and rubbed the gel around. I couldn't look at the screen, so I closed my eyes and imagined more of what Billy would be saying if he were there—"Doc, are there ways we can make the baby left-handed? Lefties are harder to pitch to"—I didn't know when I started being able to predict what Billy would say or why, even in my imagination, he annoyed me.

My thoughts were turning poisonous. I wished I had my iPod, something to help keep me steady, my mind a little fuzzy and unfocused. I was so stupid not to bring my iPod. I was about to ask Dr. Oldman if he had a CD player, a boom box—anything that could play music, any kind of music, preferably something heavy on beat, light on lyrics—when his voice cut through the air: "There! Open your eyes, see for yourself."

The image on the screen was grainy and the baby didn't look much like a baby, didn't look like a plum either. I could tell that it had a head and a body and feet, but if I squinted a little, it became nothing, a smudge on a screen.

"Everything looks great. Your baby is healthy, has toes and everything," Dr. Oldman continued. "Would you like to know the sex?"

"No." I said it too quickly.

I tried not to squint, kept my eyes wide open, struggled not to blink, stared at this thing—no, this Fully Formed Human Being—growing inside me.

"It's breathtaking, isn't it? The creation of life." Dr. Old-man looked close to tears. "These are the moments that make my job worth it."

I felt bad for all my bad thoughts about Dr. Oldman, about Billy, about everyone. I wanted to be the type of person that walked with their back straight, the dirt under their fingernails pure. I didn't want to be a chain saw, I wanted to be a plastic baggie. No shredding, just hold-ing. I wondered what animals lived under the shadows of my bones. I hoped they were animals of nobility—lions and eagles and horses with long manes—and not what I feared—vultures and wolves and drooling hyenas. I spit in a customer's pizza last week because he called me a bitch over the phone, but maybe he was having a bad day, maybe he spilled coffee on his favorite shirt, stubbed his toe, missed the bus to work, someone close to him died, maybe I really was just being a bitch.

Dr. Oldman rubbed his eyes, cleared his throat. "Sorry, you just remind me a lot of my youngest."

I thought, This is your chance, this is where you can start, ask him about his daughter, how we're alike, is her name Appalachian? I knew he wanted me to ask, I could see it in his clear brown eyes. I just smiled weakly. "It's okay. Really."

I LEFT THE CLINIC with an armful of pamphlets and a list of prenatal vitamin brands. It was only 10:00 a.m., it felt like it was 2:00 p.m., my sweating was only going to get worse. I threw the pamphlets, the list, and the ultrasound photo into the nearest trash can. I was halfway to my car when I stopped, sighed, ran back, fished out the ultrasound photo, and stuffed it into the front left pocket of my jeans.

The inside of the Festiva was boiling hot, the steering wheel hurt to touch. This was my nineteenth summer in Los Angeles. I should've known to park somewhere shaded.

I opened all the car's doors and paced in circles around it. My shift at Eddie's wasn't for over two hours and I had no idea what I was going to do with that time. Everyone I knew was always bitching about how they wanted more free time and I wanted to shove them in their chests, hard, tell them how lucky they were that each of their days contained boring, beautiful structure.

I kept replaying the last thing Dr. Oldman had said to me before I left the office. He'd hugged me tight. "Congratulations on the end of your first trimester. It's only just beginning."

He'd said it with both rows of his crooked, yellow teeth showing, said it to excite me. But the words just banged around the inside of my head and made me feel lopsided, like I was dehydrated, even though I had just finished a whole bottle of water.

I blinked hard and then opened the car's trunk, searched every corner of it. Nothing. I checked the glove box. Nothing. The overhead compartment. Nothing. I was about to give up when I reached under the driver's seat and felt my fingers brush against glass. I curled them around the body and pulled out a half-full bottle of Evan Williams.

That fucking fuck, I thought. I knew it, I fucking knew he would have a bottle stashed somewhere in here, that fucking asshole.

I took a deep swig and got into the car, turned on the radio, pulled out of the parking lot, and fiddled with the volume, started driving west. West seemed right.

I GOT TIRED OF DRIVING EVENTUALLY, pulled over about a mile from Eddie's. I still had an hour to kill and I didn't want to drink any more of Dad's bottle.

The sidewalks were busy. Unlike me, people were

dressed appropriately for summer in tank tops and shorts, their flip-flops smacked pleasantly against the pavement. I reached down and untied the laces on my sneakers, started pacing back and forth along the block.

I stared hard at every person I walked past. If they didn't tell me my shoes were untied, I cursed them in my head—Fuck you, how dare you not warn a pregnant woman that she could fall—and if they did tell me my shoes were untied, I cursed them in my head—Fuck you, leave me alone, I can do whatever I want.

I SHOWED UP FOR MY SHIFT at Eddie's soaked in sweat. My uniform polo was a dark green, and loose strands of my hair were plastered to my neck and forehead.

Darryl lowered his magazine and eyed me up and down. "You better clean up before Peter sees you. You know he's been extra bitch-ass ever since we dropped to a 'B' rating."

I shrugged. Darryl shrugged back. "Whatever," he said.

He looked back down at his magazine and added, like he'd only just remembered, "Oh, by the way, someone called asking for you. Some woman."

"A woman?" My head snapped up. "What woman?"

He raised his eyebrows, picked up a scrap of paper, and handed it to me.

I held the paper delicately in my hands, ran my fingers over the words, and repeated them softly under my breath. "Adam loved the pizza. You're amazing. Come today at 4:30 p.m. Same order. Jenny Hauser."

"So? What's all that about?" Darryl asked. "Customers

don't like you, much less use any word close to 'amazing'
to describe you."

"I'm likable and amazing, thank you." I flicked Darryl
off as I stuffed the note into my jeans pocket, the same
pocket as the ultrasound photo. "Excuse me, I have to pee."

I went to the bathroom, didn't pee. I squirted pink,
watered-down soap into my hands and scrubbed my face,
neck, arms, any sweaty exposed body parts. I combed my
hair with my fingers and tucked in my polo, untucked it,
tried to look presentable.

4

UNFORTUNATELY, it was a while before 4:30 p.m. and there were other people hungry for pizza.

A nursing home having a bingo birthday party. Two roommates, both accountants at the same firm, who were ditching work and playing Xbox in their underwear. A couple at a bar already drunk and arguing over a bag of Doritos. The lady so large that it was hard for her to get off her couch, who always hollered at me to come in—the door was unlocked, leave the pizza on the couch next to her, money was on top of the TV set. A dude who smiled and tipped well, but was certainly an asshole—no non-asshole has a lime-green Camaro. The guy who worked at the crematorium who once told me, "I like to get high and burn bodies"; he also liked pepperoni, sausage, and onions.

Fortunately, one of my favorite regulars also called in.

Rita Booker and her husband, Louie, gave me hope that

it was possible to make it into your thirties with the same person and still be in love.

They'd always answer the door together, wrapped around each other, usually minimally clothed. They barely looked at me as they paid. Rita would ask me how I was doing, how was that man of mine, wasn't life wonderful?— all while staring directly into Louie's eyes. Sometimes she would stroke my face and smile at Louie. "Look at this caramel. I hope our future babies are as pretty as she is."

When they answered the door that day, he was shirtless and in basketball shorts. She was naked underneath one of his button-downs and I could see her nipples through the soft pink material. I handed her their large Buff Bleu Chick and made sure to keep my eyes on hers.

"How's it going, girl?" Rita smiled at me, was immediately distracted by Louie nibbling on her ear. He gave me a quick grin, a wink. I knew she didn't need an answer, so I just smiled back. "That'll be $19.99."

Louie pulled a wad of bills out of his shorts and handed me a twenty plus a solid tip as Rita fixed her attention on his neck. They laughed and ran their hands over each other's bodies, searching, mapping, squeezing spots that spoke to them. I normally didn't break through their haze, just took the money and walked back to my car, but that day I had to know—"How do you guys stay so happy?"

They turned to me and their cheeks had a lovely rosy flush, and if I'd had a camera I would've snapped a picture of them right there. Once I got home, I would've stared at the photo and pulled out a set of paints, mixed until I got the exact color of their cheeks.

Louie shook the box in his one hand and played with the collar of Rita's shirt with the other. "Pizza and sex seems to help."

"Seriously, though," I said.

"I mean, we're being pretty serious." Rita looked at Louie, a stone-melting look. "Like, yeah, pizza and sex is not all it is, but when you're with someone that you love— like, really love—you work through whatever shit that's managed to stick to you over the years, and when you want to punch walls, or rip out your hair, or if you feel like if you opened your mouth only screams would come out, you remember those pizza-and-sex days."

They started kissing with tongue, so I thanked them and wished them all the best.

I CIRCLED AROUND THE BLOCK three times and still got to Jenny's house early. It was 4:23 and I didn't want to look overeager. I parked my car a few houses down and put the radio's volume at 10, 11, 12, back to 11, stared at the clock.

4:24

The song that was on the radio said the word "release," over and over. The drumbeat was too aggressive and I felt it weirdly in my elbows and knees. I changed the station and focused on making my thoughts unfocused.

4:25

A Christian Rock station. The song wasn't annoying, wasn't saying anything like "I love you, God. You are every-thing, God. God likes his steak rare." The song was slow and soft, not many lyrics, just a few "Hallelujahs" exhaled here and there.

4:26

Would I ever carry a briefcase? How many times in a row did you have to listen to a song you loved before it became a song you liked hearing every now and then? Is it only called a nervous breakdown if there's someone there to point at you and be, like, "Yo, get your shit straight, you are nervous and you are breaking down"? The heart of a shrimp is located in its head.

4:28

Dad used to carry a briefcase, even when he was working jobs like graveyard-shift mall security, office janitor, mover—and there was an odd stint when he had a paper route—he'd put his briefcase into the bike's front basket as he cruised around the neighborhood tossing the L.A. *Times* into people's front yards.

The briefcase never had much in it: a sci-fi paperback, a few sheets of paper, pens stolen from dentists' offices and car dealerships, jelly beans. Dad would put a couple green ones in my hand, my favorite, and say, "You need the briefcase. People don't take you seriously without the briefcase. How would it look if I was walking around with just a pack of jelly beans in my hand?"

4:30

I got out of the car and hit the lock button twice, started walking toward Jenny's house.

▼

I ONLY HAD TO KNOCK ONCE before the door swung open and a little boy in dirt-stained clothes answered.

We stared at each other and I tried to think of something to say, but I found quiet children to be strange, unnatural. I would've been less alarmed if he'd answered the door hopping up and down, screaming. He just stood there, staring, mouth closed and tight; even his blinks seemed solemn.

We were saved by Jenny sliding into view, nearly falling over. "I forgot how slippery these floors get when you're wearing socks." She hugged me, and I was rigid for a moment, shocked by the easy intimacy, and then I leaned into it and breathed deep. "I see you've met the most beautiful boy in the world. I swear, he's not usually this dirty. He just got home from baseball practice." She ruffled his hair. "This is Adam."

Adam remained staring. His eyes were the same shade of brown as Jenny's. "Adam," Jenny said, "can you thank this nice lady for the pizza? Remember how good it was last week?"

"It was okay," he said. "Thank you, though."

My chest twisted at this muted, muttered thank-you. A part of me wanted to shake the kid, change his face, and the other felt achy, bruised, a flash of recognition and fear. I remembered being a quiet little kid, constantly aware and uncomfortable with the ways grown-ups talked to me, how much they seemed to want from me.

Jenny took the pizza and handed me another too-much tip. "So—how're you doing? You look a little more worn out than the last time I saw you."

"I'm doing okay," I said, wondering if my equally bland response would catch Adam's attention, warm him to me.

"Well," Jenny said, "if you're not, there's a support group that meets every Thursday at eight-thirty p.m. at that little church between the hardware store and the dough-nut shop. It's for expecting moms and current struggling moms. They used to be two separate groups, but they joined them together after funding was cut. The group isn't bad, and there's always hot, fresh cookies."

I almost told her that the church was Catholic and called Holy Name of Jesus, and that the cookies weren't fresh, just microwaved before the group started. I didn't want to talk about how I knew that, though, the many afternoons I'd spent there listening to strangers grieve.

She put the pizza down and took my hand in one of hers, Adam's in the other. We formed a chain. "Please come. I go every week, and some of these women are just nasty. I need a friend."

I looked at Adam and, I can't be sure, I thought I saw him nod. Just once, not even a nod, a slight tilt of the head. I knew what it meant—"Go, watch, protect her."

"Okay," I said. "I'll be there."

5

MOM AND BILLY ooh-ed and aww-ed as they stared at the crumpled ultrasound photo. I stood by the fridge, alternating between eating strips of cold chicken and scooping peanut butter with my fingers straight from the jar and into my mouth.

My lower-back pain had worsened during the last hour of my shift and I was starving for something, anything, other than pizza. I'd gotten home and immediately dropped my bag to the floor and lain across the couch. Mom was talking about making me a hot meal, something with rice and veggies, a little hot sauce, when Billy asked to see the baby's first photo. After I pulled it out of my pocket, they swiped it from my hands and began smoothing out its edges. Soon, they were huddled together on the couch, admiring the photo like the secrets of the universe existed in the profile of this fruit-sized creation—which maybe they did, and I was just blind.

I dipped a piece of chicken directly into the peanut

butter and watched the two of them together. Billy's arm was around Mom's shoulder and she was leaning into his side. The cat Billy had brought home, whose name I didn't care to remember, was on the couch, the top half of its body in Billy's lap, the bottom half on Mom's. They were talking loudly at each other—"You see that, Mom? That's the Bradley family chin!," "Those little feet! Think of how they'll grow and all the places they'll carry him," "I can already tell he's got a good sense of humor"—I had a vision of them six months from now in the same position on the couch, except instead of a picture, they were cradling and cooing at a bundle of blue blankets. Even the cat would be involved, meows and coos mixing together.

It was so easy to close my eyes and see Mom feeding baby food she boiled and mashed up herself because she didn't trust big-name brands, "That Gerber baby freaks me out." Billy crawling on the carpet with Baby, pretending to be a tiger, dinosaur, semitruck, some large, roaring creature. Mom singing to Baby as she folded laundry, Korean lullabies and Joan Jett. Billy changing Baby's diaper while reading him words out of the dictionary: "'Abide: uh-byde, verb, to bear patiently, to endure without yielding, to wait for, to accept without objection, to remain stable or fixed in a state, to continue in place.'" Mom and Billy on the couch again, Baby between them, TV on, but they're looking down at him softly, with care.

It was so easy to close my eyes and see them, but I could never conjure myself into those scenes. No mashing, feeding, crawling, roaring, folding, singing, diaper changing, reading—I was never snuggled into the couch with them. I stood watching them with a hunk of peanut butter and chicken in my mouth and wondered if I would spend the next eighteen years standing there.

It took me a moment to realize that Mom and Billy had started talking about me.

"I miss when she was a baby, you know," Mom said. "Her dad, rest his soul, was busy all the time trying to write and make money. He'd leave for hours, sometimes days. The house would always be so empty. I used to just walk from room to room, touching the walls. Sometimes I'd go to the store and buy different paints and test them out— Cornflower, Seafoam, Mango, did you know there's a shade of purple called Fandango?

"Then, one day, she was born and the house wasn't empty anymore. She filled every inch of it. She took up all my time. I stopped buying paints. There's a reason the house's walls are Goldenrod now—it's the color I painted the house two days before she was born."

Billy hugged Mom and said something that I couldn't hear—I was running past them to the bathroom. I had a second to appreciate that someone had just cleaned the toilet, the water was blue, toilet-water blue might've been my favorite color. The next second, I was throwing up.

I'd thrown up many times before I got pregnant—when I was fourteen and worried my face would be round and chubby forever, during a party where I was debating losing my virginity to the boy in my pre-calc class who smelled like Old Spice and Doritos, after Dad told me that all his best memories were before I was born, stomach flus, gas-station burritos—but now I got no relief as I emptied myself into that pretty blue toilet water.

I felt Billy's hands kneading my shoulders, Mom's gathering my hair and holding it back. They whispered soothing things into my ears until I finished. I lightly pushed away Billy's hands when he tried to wipe the puke from my mouth with a tissue and did it myself, with the back of my hand.

BILLY SHOULD'VE BEEN GOING to USC in the fall.

When he first got accepted, everyone thought that he got in because of baseball, that he was going to be the Trojans' newest relief pitcher. This frustrated him. "I love baseball, but I'm really not that good. Like, I'm the best at our high school, but that doesn't mean much. A lot of people are the best at their high school. Besides, I can do more than just throw things and sweat." He'd say this frowning, un-frowning, trying to keep the irritation out of his voice and failing.

Along with being the best baseball player at our shitty high school, Billy also had a near-perfect grade point average and SAT score, did nice things like volunteer for organizations that made him spend his weekends picking chip bags and empty beer cans off beaches and reading to old people in rooms with lighting that made everything look sadder, closer to death. USC had given Billy a full academic scholarship; the baseball coach had no idea who he was.

Billy believed in video games. He talked often about how

they got a bad rep, that people used adjectives like "sense-less," "frivolous," "mind-numbing," to describe them. But what was wrong with mind-numbing? What was wrong with wanting to stop moving every once in a while, with wanting just to sit on your couch and let your head drain as you thought about nothing except racing along Rain-bow Road, killing Nazi Zombies, how there were over 150 Pokémon to catch. His big plan was to major in game design and create a video game called The Helpful Sheep.

"Explain it to me again. What's the point of The Helpful Sheep?" I would ask, even though I knew exactly what the point was. I just liked hearing Billy talk about it. His eyes would widen and his hands would move all over the place. He liked gesturing, consciously or unconsciously, pairing words with sharp slices and punches to the air.

"So, okay, it's very simple. It's exactly what the title promises." His hands would move separately—right slice, left punch. "You're a sheep who lives in a studio apartment in a major nondescript city. You wake up every day and eat a bowl of fresh-cut grass and milk. After scrubbing your hooves and washing your wool, you trot out your front door and provide people with everything they want and need, hate asking for—free, unsolicited help." Generally, I kissed him around this time. He would always need a minute after, to wipe his lips and smile bashfully, before continuing his rant. "The game is free-roam. You can go anywhere you want in the city. It doesn't matter where you go—everywhere there are people that need your help."

"What kind of help?"

"Any kind. Let's say a guy—we'll call him Doug—is making a sandwich and it's all looking good. Doug's got the ham, Doug's got the cheese, whole-wheat bread, lettuce, tomato, ketchup, mustard, mayo, maybe a strip of bacon for a crunch. Before he pops the sandwich on his Foreman Grill, he decides he wants an extra salty bite. He needs pickles. He goes to the fridge and pulls out a jar of Vlasics." Another kiss, with tongue. "Fuck! The jar won't open. The folks at Vlasic are serious about keeping their shit air-tight fresh! What do you do? What can you do? Do you just throw out the sandwich? Order Beef and Broccoli, hold the broccoli, from Panda? Nah, fuck that, you're so close. It's time for *The Helpful Sheep*."

Billy often stood up at this point. Both hands above his head, quick punches. "As the sheep, you can fix problems like this. You can open Doug's pickle jar, save his lunch from being bland. After that, you can walk next door and scrub in and around Mrs. Wilson's toilet bowl. She was a basketball player in her youth, her knees are wrecked, you're eliminating so much pain from her life. Li'l Susie across the street is sad that she's the only one of her friends that doesn't know how to ride a bike. You can help her get off those training wheels and not feel left out! The sheep accepts no payment for these services, just hugs."

Flopping back on the bed, he'd wrap me in his arms, press sloppy wet kisses wherever he could reach. "I'm telling you, babe. This game is it. It'll reduce stress, encourage people to be kinder to others."

"How does a sheep open a jar without thumbs? And it's going to be a cartoon sheep, right? Cartoon sheep are much cuter than the real thing."

I missed these conversations. Shortly after we found out about the pregnancy, Billy called USC to let them know that he wouldn't be attending that fall. I told Billy that it was okay, that he should go be a student and kick ass, live in the dorms, and drive home on the weekends to see me and the baby. He wouldn't budge, though, kept repeating that he didn't want to miss anything. He told me with a tightness in his voice that he didn't want the baby to grow up and feel about him what he felt about his parents. "Our kid is going to grow up wondering about a lot of things. Never, though, will he wonder if I'm going to be home for dinner. I will always be there to wonder with him."

We stopped talking about USC and The Helpful Sheep.

I WATCHED BILLY'S BACK as he undressed for bed. I knew I wanted to start a fight. I also knew that I hated fighting, hated how ugly I felt and was sure I looked when I screamed. I waited until he was down to his underwear and one sock before I stood up, grabbed his dick firmly between my hands.

"I need you to fuck me. Hard."

This always got him going. Not the part about fucking, not even the idea about fucking hard. The word "need." It was a sexy word. "Want" was something you applied to new CDs by your favorite bands, the desire to ditch class and smoke weed on the beach, deep-tissue massages, five-ply toilet paper, 24/7 A/C, guac that was a full dollar extra. "Need" was reserved for things like air, water, sleep, shits that cleaned out your insides, the stuff that kept you breathing. Billy was hard before we kissed. All my clothes were still on.

My bed creaked loudly if you so much as flipped from your right side to your left. We had a system. We'd grab all the dirty clothes from our laundry basket and toss them on the floor. On top of the clothes, we'd spread out a ratty old towel I'd gotten for free from a Dodgers game Dad took me to when I was nine. If we had trouble keeping quiet, there was a meaty part between neck and shoulder that didn't hurt too bad if bitten; fingers could be sucked on too.

We quickly threw down the clothes, the blanket, ourselves on top of it. Billy sneezed twice into my mouth. An old gym sock got tangled in my hair. He told me that he loved the smell of my new perfume. I told him I wasn't wearing perfume, just Speed Stick. We laughed and made marks on each other's bodies, wet red spots that even after they dried would still shine for days afterward, make us smile whenever we saw them reflected back in mirrors and windows, little red beacons that screamed to whoever stared at them, "Hey, hi, hello, howdy, look at me, I am alive and loved." Billy pushed inside of me and I moaned against his neck, made the first red mark above his collarbone.

I was enjoying myself and feeling grateful for that fact. I was lucky and I knew it. He came quickly, before I could, and I didn't mind. I kind of preferred it, actually—feeling him pull out and fall onto his back, knowing that I made him feel good, happy we could just lie there now, no talking, the only sounds his satisfied panting, the whirring of our two fans, the TV from downstairs, either the news or a game show—Mom liked both.

Billy being Billy, the silence didn't last long.

"You didn't? Did you?"

"No," I said. "But it's okay."

Billy, also being Billy, hated when he came and I didn't. To him it was unfair, unjust, his world would remain unbalanced until I had also had an orgasm of equal, toe-curling magnitude. He ignored my assurances that everything was all good, really, and hopped back on top of me, started kissing my neck and moving lower and lower. He did have a nice tongue, used the right amount of teeth and suction. I ran my hands up and down the sides of his face and each time I got to his ears, I thought about wrapping my fingers around them and yanking him back to my eye level, grabbing his chin, and telling him to fucking stop.

It wasn't that I had trouble saying no. It was just that sometimes saying no wouldn't solve anything and would lead to longer conversations, ones that I wasn't prepared to have.

Like, if I told Billy, "No, please stop," I would also have to tell him that lately I'd been having trouble orgasming. And if I told him that, then he'd ask with deep, aching sincerity, "Interesting, why do you think you are unable to reach orgasm?" And to answer that question I'd have to breathe and speak words that were painful even to think.

Usually, I'd masturbate every morning in the shower or in those quiet sections of the day when no one was home and books and music and TV and eating and sweating and pacing up and down the stairs and everything else that filled my time at home, all of it, seemed dull. However, the past few weeks, each time I tried, the minutes would just stack on top of each other until I was so frustrated that I'd hop out of the shower or roll off my bed, body tight, fists clenched and ready to hit something.

We'd had sex more times than I could count, and I didn't have any idea what I used to think about during. I should've written it down somewhere word for word, on colorful note cards, yellow or pink, bright squares I could pull out whenever I needed release. It was too easy for my mind to wander. The smallest things would distract me. I'd be starting to feel good and then my eyes would focus on something, anything, and I would spiral.

An old orange peel peeking out of the trash can would make me wonder what I tasted like. Was it something distinct and nameable? If someone kissed me would they later tell their buddies how my lips were orangey? Probably not, it was probably something unfruity, how could you taste like anything unless you were constantly eating it? Best-case, I had burrito lips. My desk lamp would be on and it would make no sense to me—I rarely sat there anymore, hadn't picked up a book since I don't know when, there was no need for extra light. The one, two, three, four water glasses scattered on random surfaces around my room—one glass, I could've just used one. The sound of a car screeching to a halt outside, honking, angry voices, I knew it was because of that fucking palm tree—tall, an obnoxiously thick trunk, it blocked the stop sign in front of my house and caused near accidents all the time. My sheets were a pleasant shade of blue, but had been washed so many times that there were patches where the blue was less vibrant, there was no way to get the original color back. In the shower, I'd pick a water droplet on the wall, name it, and watch it plummet to its death. Closing my eyes didn't help. I could conjure all sorts of images against the darkness of my lids.

I tugged lightly on Billy's ears. I kept my gaze firmly on his forehead as he went down on me. Any higher, I risked seeing something that would distract me. Any lower, I could be in danger of making eye contact with him.

I started picturing myself in other places. I didn't intend to, it just happened. I was watching the mole above Billy's right eyebrow, closed my eyes for a moment, and then I was sitting cross-legged in the outfield of a baseball stadium. No time to see who was playing or winning—soon I was in the supermarket with Dad, slapping watermelons, trying to guess which was the sweetest. Next, my high school ceramics studio. Not creating any bowls or plates or mugs, just running the dark red clay through my fingers. I was still holding the clay when I looked up, found myself lying on a couch next to an empty bag of Hot Cheetos, a half-eaten salad, a tub of cream cheese. The floor was covered in old T-shirts. I was surrounded by seven chairs, seven shitty paintings. I threw the clay away, or maybe I wasn't even holding it anymore—I wanted to see Jenny Hauser.

It wasn't a sex fantasy. I didn't picture her hands or mouth on me, although I won't pretend those images disgusted me. I was just lying on her couch and wishing that the Hot Cheetos bag wasn't empty, that a pillow was under my head, that she had a little music on, something with lyrics that made you think and hurt with a beat that made you want to dance. She walked into the room right as Billy started sucking on my clit.

"You like that?" Billy asked.

"Yes," I said, pushing his head back down. "Don't stop."

Her ponytail was loose and low and her shirt was wrinkled, the same stain on its collar. She walked from painting to painting until, in front of the fifth one, the turtle she didn't give to me, she collapsed.

I carried her back to the couch. I stroked her face, pushed away the loose strands of her hair, and tucked them behind her ears. When she opened her eyes, she smiled at me. "Thank you," she said. "I've been on my feet all day."

"You're welcome."

"I'm really thirsty."

A glass of water appeared in my left hand. I gave it to her. She drank the whole thing in one clean gulp.

"You're wonderful," Jenny said. "Do you believe me? You're wonderful."

She stared at me. I stared back.

"I believe you," I said.

I came hard, grabbing Billy's ears tight and pulling him into me. I squeezed my eyes shut, tried not to leave Jenny or the living room, but I couldn't will myself back, only random spots and patterns of color would flash across the dark of my lids.

"Wow," Billy said. He crawled out from between my legs and lay next to me, wrapped his arms around me. "That was incredible."

"Yeah," I said, patting his back. I wanted to get out of

bed and run to Dad's shed, turn the TV on mute, chug a beer, and spend the rest of the night masturbating with my eyes closed.

I didn't get up, didn't go to the shed, not until much later, and then only for twenty minutes, to sip half a beer and watch an infomercial about shower curtains that were also picture frames, Popsicles with tiny flecks of kale in them, other necessary vitamins. I continued patting Billy's back. My room's ceiling was blank and white with no cracks. It was a good backdrop for me to project my thoughts and feelings onto and attempt to sort them into something resembling order and sense. "Incredible," I said.

6

WE WERE LEGALLY REQUIRED to log a break each shift. Luckily, we weren't legally required to eat the pizza during our break. Eddie's pizza wasn't great, but it wasn't terrible. It was just hard to eat the same thing every day, no matter what it was.

There was a taco truck Darryl and I liked that sat in the gas station parking lot across the street. We'd go at least three times a week. The salsa and guac were a little watery, but free. We'd wrap up a few slices with various toppings and make a trade with the guy in the truck, whom we simply called Taco Man. He knew we called him that too. Once, in a show of goodwill, Darryl asked for his real name in bad middle-school Spanish, and he just smirked. "Taco Man is fine." Five slices of pizza got us three tacos each. This total was decided on with zero discussion and no one ever complained.

Peter had hired a new guy the week before. His name was Willie and he was at least forty, had neon-green braces and an intense love of show tunes. A good worker and a genuinely nice person, he drove Darryl and me absolutely fucking nuts.

We wished we liked him more, we really did. However, some days, he was just too much. He'd be singing something from *Guys and Dolls* as he scraped gum off the bottoms of the tables, and Darryl would turn to me and clear his throat, twice. "So—how's Granny Mavis doing?" My dad's mom was dead and named Dorothy and my mom's mom I'd never met and only knew by a string of Korean expletives. Granny Mavis was no one, a code for "Willie is fucking killing me, and if we don't get the fuck out of here I'll fucking kill him—I'm fucking hungry." "Granny is good," I would say. "Her diaper just needs to be changed a lot."

Darryl would get different kinds of tacos each time. I only ever got the *al pastor*. Since I didn't get it every day, each bite was always perfect. We'd lean against the gas pumps and scarf them down like starving rats.

"We should be nicer to Willie," I said, sucking the grease off my thumb. "I hate how he looks whenever we go to lunch together. We at least have to bring him something back."

"I know, I know." Darryl pulled out a plastic water bottle of liquid I didn't question. He took a long swig. "He just makes me think of high school."

"What? You weren't popular in high school?"

"I was a fat black faggot in band," he snorted. "What do you think?"

I wiped my lips on a napkin. "I didn't know you played an instrument."

"Yup. Trumpet."

I started pulling at the napkin's edges. "So," I said, "you knew you were gay back then."

"Yeah, I tried not to think much about it. Looking back, though, it was obvious."

"How was it obvious?"

"It's hard to explain." Darryl began crumpling his napkin, making it a tight round ball. "I found and still find girls attractive, but only boys can ruin my life."

I wanted to ask him for a pull from his water bottle. I watched a loose drop move down the side and nearly leaned over and licked it up. "I had this girlfriend back then," Darryl continued. "Sweet girl, Maggie Tyler. I mentioned once that apples were my favorite fruit, and the next day she showed up at my locker with a paper bag full of the biggest, juiciest McIntoshes I'd ever seen. And she didn't work at the grocery store or nothing. She bought me those with her own money. My mom liked her too, especially that she was a tiny, pretty white girl."

"But?"

He laughed. "But, the entire time she was bringing me bags of apples and charming my mom, I was filling notebooks with the name of the boy who sat next to me in woodshop."

"What was his name?"

"Jeremy Durant. He had a chin dimple and the smoothest hands. Made these beautiful oak steps so that his little dog, a Frenchie named Beyoncé, could get onto his bed all by herself."

"Wow, now I have a crush on him."

"Don't." He sighed, threw the napkin on the ground. "Once I filled a couple notebooks, I convinced myself that he felt the same way and that I should tell him. Predictably, it went terribly, and he told the whole school that trumpets weren't the only things that I blew. Maggie told my mom. I came home that day to them holding each other and sobbing. My main thought when I saw Maggie was 'Damn, I'm going to have to buy my own apples now.'"

I picked up his napkin and threw it into the trash can. "I'm sorry."

"Don't be. He's a fool and I still think he's gay. Like, his dog's name was Beyoncé."

"But how did you know? Like, how did you even know Jeremy was someone you could like?"

"Why dudes? I don't know. Nature, nurture, who the fuck knows. The outcome is the same." He looked up toward the sky. I looked up with him. Pure blue, not a cloud in sight. "Why Jeremy? Another question with another answer I'm not sure of. It doesn't seem like we get to choose who we like. I wish we could, it would all be a lot simpler if I could just decide to like someone. If I could, I'd choose Maggie Tyler every damn day. Everything would be easier, my chest wouldn't feel like it does now, like there's something rotting inside of it. I would have an apple with breakfast, lunch, dinner."

He looked back down. I kept looking up. There was a plane in the sky and I was trying to guess how many people were inside it. I pictured every seat, every person, and I wondered about their names, ages, jobs, what they were listening to on their iPods, where they were coming from,

who they were going home to. I hoped they all had someone waiting for them at the airport who'd smile at them
the second they walked into Baggage Claim, who'd hug
them and tell them they missed them and really mean it.
Someone who'd drive them home and ask them all about
their trip, let them crack open their chest and dump the
weight of their day inside.

"Sorry, I'm being a downer," Darryl said. I looked back at
him. He plastered an almost believable smile on his face.
"Tell me about your boyfriend. Billy, right? I remember
that one time he dropped by just to say hey, just because
he missed you. He's no Jeremy. He'll be a good daddy."

"Yeah, he's the best," I said.

Darryl stared at my belly. "Can I touch?"

I grabbed the bottle from his hand and took a swig, leaving barely another mouthful. "No."

SOMETIMES PEOPLE I went to high school with called in.

At best, it was awkward. They'd open the door and, no
matter how long it took them to place me, when they
did, their smiles would fall for a second. The next second,
their smiles would be back and forced, acting like we were
meeting on purpose and not because they were hungry
and about to pay me. They'd try to hug me, shout, "Class
of 2011!" I'd pretend I would be open to hugging if only I
wasn't holding the pizza they ordered. I'd offer them their
box in one hand, hold out the open palm of my other for
money, hoping to end the interaction as quickly as pos-

sible. They'd ignore my moves and ask me if it was true about the baby. After the first few times, I stopped asking how they'd heard about it—everyone was friends with or had a friend that was friends with Billy, had bumped into him over the past two weeks, and had heard him gush about the baby and everything he had planned. They loved talking about how brave I was, that people could fuck off if they didn't approve, their sister's friend's sister was pregnant out of high school, baby socks were the cutest things in the whole world. What they were doing in the fall inevitably came next.

"And I really think that majoring in communications at Cal State Long Beach is going to be a great start to the rest of my adult life."

"Totally."

"What're you doing?"

"I don't know."

It seemed as if there was nothing more uncomfortable that I could say. They could support a teenage pregnancy, but not this, not a person who drifted from one moment to the next without any idea about where she was headed. Their smiles would fall again, longer this time, they'd need to look away for a moment to recover. When they turned back, they'd stare at the bridge of my nose, the gap between my eyebrows, the center of my forehead, anywhere but my eyes, a place where their own insecurities might be reflected back to them, murky in the brown of my irises. "That's so cool," they would mumble in my direction, might cough or rub the side of their arm, lace their fingers together. "That's so cool." Another pause. "So—how much do I owe you?" On my walk back to my car, they'd shout out to say hi to Billy.

It was worse when they didn't remember me at all.

They'd open the door and look at me like we'd never passed each other in hallways, drunk from the same low-pressure water fountains, copied off each other's tests, laughed at teachers that didn't care, laughed at teachers that cared too much, seen each other at the Burger King where you could buy cheap weed. Stanley Luna told me once at a party that I had a killer rack. Standing on his doorstep with two boxes of Extra Sausage, Extra Cheese, Normal Sauce, he barely looked up from his phone, quickly thrust bills and a few coins into my hand, said, "Thanks much," while closing the door.

Whether they remembered or didn't remember me, I'd take the long route back to Eddie's. No matter how loud I turned up the radio, I couldn't avoid thinking about one fact—even if I wasn't pregnant, I would be in the exact same place I was now.

Billy used to lie in bed filling out college applications on his laptop. I'd lie next to him, hands behind my head, eyes closed, the clacking of his keyboard soothing me, putting me into the state on the edge of sleep.

"When're you going to fill out your applications?"

Eyes open. "I don't know."

"What do you think you'd want to do once you graduate?"

I'd shrug or try to change the conversation. "Let's go to Taco Bell."

"Well, what do you like doing?"

This was the most painful question he could ask, maybe because I knew how I would answer it—I liked eating cereal early in the morning on the front steps of the house, seeing how sure and confident Mom's hands moved when she folded laundry, watching TV on mute while I listened to my iPod, reading under trees and watching sunlight leak through the leaves above and cast strange patterns on my skin and the pages, pulling off my jeans the minute I got home, Gummy Bears, I liked after we fucked, when we just lay in each other's arms, not speaking—none of these answers were what he was looking for.

I never applied to any colleges, never was able to answer the question of my future purpose with anything other than the three words that'd made my former classmates squirm, made Billy frown and try to coax ideas out of me.

"Think of things you're good at," Billy would say. "Think of people you admire and the work they did, think about what mark you'd want to leave behind on the world." Mom never minded my answer much, would hug me and tell me I had all the time in the world to decide, I could do all my deciding from the comfort of home and the room I'd slept in every night of my life.

"I don't know."

After a few deliveries, I realized my classmates thought I'd started working at Eddie's as a result of the pregnancy, but I'd been working there for two weeks before I found out. Billy was talking constantly about USC, the community colleges nearby that I could take classes at that would inspire me; he bought a sweatshirt for himself, a bear for mom and me with words on its belly, "Someone Who Loves

Me Goes to USC." Meanwhile, I asked every person I was even slightly friends with if they knew of places hiring.

My old lab partner, Gina Ward, got me an interview at Eddie's. I put on one of two button-downs I owned and pants without rips in them and sat across from her uncle Peter. I thought the interview went well, but didn't hear back for over a week. I asked Gina at lunch one day if Peter had told her anything and she said, "Dude, you fucked up."

"What do you mean?"

"Peter said you came in wearing a wrinkled shirt, the look in your eyes made him nervous."

"What look?"

"Vacant, a little corpsey."

"Corpsey?"

"As in 'corpse' with a 'y.' As in, you looked like a dead body."

"Ah."

I got the job because Gina begged him to give it to me. The first week I did my best to do everything he taught me perfectly. I mopped floors and wiped counters and drove to every address as quickly as I could without speeding. I sometimes thought about my life after summer, but mostly just mopped and wiped and drove and focused on little details directly in front of me. Finally, I had something to do after the final school bell rang.

The dull shine of clean linoleum counters, the gleam of wet floors, pizza smelled good, the dividing lines of the streets were better to stare at than clouds, there were no pictures to be seen in them, just dashes and lines of yellow and white, all the same, another job I could be good at—

crouching low, inhaling asphalt and paint, flicking a brush straight and even, over and over.

I WASN'T RELIGIOUS AND THOUGHT anyone who said "Amen" seriously and not just as a way to blend in at church or to please someone else's parents before dinner was weird. But every time I stood inside a church, I felt something bend in my chest.

It could've been how even small churches felt massive, how, when you stood and looked up at the high ceilings, you felt like you were about to be swallowed up by something bigger and greater than you were and later, when you emerged, blinking, you'd be bigger and greater. The cross was a simple symbol, a weighty one. Whether on the tip-top of a church's steeple or plastered on the bumper of a pickup truck, you felt its quiet stare of judgment. Stone angels were impossible to make eye contact with.

I think it was the stained glass. Lots of things were massive, judgment was all around, I could walk with my head down, staring only at the rubber toes of my sneakers, but stained glass demanded to be viewed. I liked how the colors were both bright and dark, colors I would've happily bathed in. As if the colors weren't enough, church's stained-glass windows always had a picture within them. Men, women, children, animals, trees, sometimes just geometric patterns—the stained glass made them holy. I wished stained-glass windows were everywhere, not just churches. How lovely a McDonald's would be if you could order a Big Mac while being surrounded by stained glass.

I stood on the sidewalk in front of the Holy Name of Jesus Church on the Thursday after I'd seen Jenny again and, for what felt like the million-and-tenth time, dabbed my forehead dry with the front of my shirt. To the left, the hardware store's windows were dark, the owner and his friends, equally male, middle-aged, hairy everywhere except the tops of their heads, sitting on chairs outside drinking forties, passing a joint and the L.A. Times back and forth, exhaling smoke and yelling about the daily fuck-ups. The doughnut shop was lit, but empty except for the dead-eyed, moppy-haired dude texting behind the counter and the homeless woman sleeping in a booth in the back, near the restroom, clinging to her bulging garbage bag like it was full of precious jewels or cherished memories and not just dirty, dented cans. I dabbed my forehead again. It felt like a mistake to be there.

After my shift ended, I'd asked Darryl to make a call and lie for me on his phone. Together, we called Mom and told her that I'd be coming home late, I was going to Darryl's house and we were going to eat pizza and watch a documentary about Jackie Kennedy. She liked hearing that I had friends and thought the former first lady was gorgeous and graceful and that Marilyn Monroe was a no-talent whore. We hung up the phone and Darryl frowned at me, but just said, "See you tomorrow?"

"See you tomorrow."

Inside the church, the air was even warmer than it was outside. I didn't want to go back outside, though, was worried I might start running toward my car, or even past it— how many miles would it take for my legs to give up and crumple against my will? I sat in one of the pews in the back and pulled my iPod out of my pocket, put the volume so low I had to work to hear it.

I hadn't been inside the church for over a year, since my last Grief and Loss of a Loved One meeting. Billy and I had been fucking for two weeks at that point and didn't think there was anything more we could get from the meetings. As I sat in that pew fiddling with my iPod's volume, I asked myself for the first time if that decision was the wrong one.

What if those meetings were it? What if those meetings would've saved me? Maybe if I had kept going to those meetings I would've learned all the answers to all the questions I had. Like: Where am I going and how do I get there? What have I done and what will I continue to do? Will I ever wake up and look in the mirror and feel good about the person staring back at me? Another thought entered my mind, and I hated it the minute it did, but once it was conjured it was impossible not to repeat and repeat and repeat—what if going to those meetings would've stopped me from getting pregnant?

My favorite stained-glass window in the church was a small one. It was oval and centered right behind the altar. A man kneeling before a sun. His arms outstretched. The man was probably Jesus and he was probably praying, but I chose to ignore those things—you didn't have to be religious to love the sun and the way it felt against your skin, to have a moment so beautiful and pure that it brought you to your knees.

"You came."

I turned around and ripped the headphones out of my ears. Jenny was standing there with an armful of roses. She looked like she'd jumped out of a scene of a bad rom-com. This was the third time I'd seen her and, like the previous two times, she looked tired, slightly out of breath, like she'd spent the whole day in constant motion. She was sweating more than even me. I wondered when the last time she sat down was and for how long. I hoped that I'd just seen her on three tough days. I wanted to pat her forehead dry with the front of my shirt.

"Do you have a hot date or something?"

"Huh?"

I pointed to the roses and she looked down at them and laughed. "Oh, right. Well, on my bike ride over here I saw the owner of a corner store throwing heaps of roses into the dumpster. Guess how long a flower lives after the stem has been cut."

"I don't know."

"Ten days. And that's best-case. Like, ten days even if you're keeping it in a nice vase and watering properly and often." She sat down next to me and I was happy to see her off her feet. "Ten fucking days. What a life. Doesn't that just break your heart a little bit?"

We'd never sat next to each other before. She'd hugged me twice, but there was something more intimate about being close to someone and not touching. I could've counted the number of hairs on her arm if I'd wanted to and I kind of did. I imagined us lying in a meadow, even though I'd never been to a meadow and had no idea how to find one. It was just nice to picture and I liked the idea of us lying somewhere together outdoors, the smell of grass, no clocks, just me and her, counting hairs until it was too dark to see.

Jenny shoved a rose in my face. "Please take one. Give it a good home for however many days left it's got to live."

THE MEETING was in the church's basement, the same room as before. The walls were a different color, though, a bright red. I couldn't tell if I liked it or not, if it was warm and inviting or aggressive and exhausting. I also wasn't sure exactly what color the walls were last year. I just knew they weren't red.

The women at the meeting varied in ages and belly sizes. There was a woman who looked too old to be a mom, hair curly and pure white, the bones in her hands looked thin and crushable. One girl even younger than me, skinny everywhere except her very pregnant stomach, which peeked out of her tight shirt and hung over the belt of her jeans. She made eye contact with me and I knew she'd been a freshman last year. Another looked to be in her mid-twenties, and the way she smiled often and wide and how she kept her hands constantly on top of her belly made me sure that this was her first child. Most women were Jenny's age, soft midsections and sagging upper arms, but none had a ponytail close to her length. Some had wedding rings, a lot did not. No one seemed to be in charge. We all just sat on colorful plastic chairs arranged in a circle, and after a beat, someone started talking, then another, then another. When someone finished speaking, we thanked her by first name and clapped. Those who clapped the loudest and hardest generally talked the longest. I tried to clap long and hard too, even though I wasn't planning on speaking. My palms ached after the second speaker.

"I have a new baby, an old beagle, and a boyfriend who's bad at wiping—there's shit everywhere."

"I hate the way everyone talks to me at work now. They just ask endless questions about Sam. It's like they forgot I used to ride a Harley and host poker night."

"He already wants another one. I can't tell if it's because he actually wants another kid or if he just wants me and my huge tits to stay at home longer."

"Is it wrong if I rock the baby to sleep with rap music? Will that affect her SAT scores?"

"Just because I have blue hair doesn't mean I'm going to be a bad mother."

The rose Jenny gave me was thornless and fit neatly in my front left jeans pocket. I kept pulling it out and twirling it between my fingers as the women talked. Everything they said made me want to offer them a drink. A bottle of tequila would go quick here.

A woman gripping a Styrofoam cup of coffee tightly between both her hands: "Does anyone hear phantom crying?" The rest of the women blinked, a couple looked to their left, right, shrugged. She blinked twice. "Like, I'll be chopping carrots, or going through the mail, taking a shower, and then, all of a sudden, I hear Daisy crying. I'll hear it and my heart will stop for a second and then, the next second, it's beating so hard the only thing I can hear above the beating is the crying.

"I'll tell myself it's not real or that, even if it is real, it's okay, babies cry. But what if it is real? And what if it's not just normal crying, what if something is really wrong? So, whatever I'm doing, I'll stop. Dinner never gets cooked, bills're thrown on the carpet, I'll run out of the shower without a towel, and most of the time she's just fine, lying in her crib and chewing on her stuffed bear. But some-times she's crying, and I hate that I prefer those times, that I'll see her little face all red and wet and miserable, but I'm just relieved that I didn't make it up."

She takes a shaky sip of her coffee. "The worst is when I'm running errands or at work and Daisy is nowhere near. I just have to keep walking or keep typing, saying, She's okay, she's okay, she's okay, until the sound goes away."

The room was quiet. Everyone looked around, hoping for someone to break the silence. Finally, a woman whose name started with either an "H" or a "P" said loudly, bring-ing her hands together, "Thank you, Melissa. Thank you so much for your bravery."

I slowly began clapping along with everyone else and, for the first time, made eye contact with Jenny. She stared at me, strained, uncomfortable, and I didn't know what to do other than watch her until she looked away.

OUTSIDE AFTER THE MEETING some of the women gath-ered in mini-circles and chatted before they drove off or husbands, boyfriends, people who watched out for them, came to pick them up from the curb. I stood alone at the top of the church steps, trying to see where Jenny went.

I didn't see her in any of the mom circles and didn't expect to. She was the first one out of her seat once the meeting ended, taking the stairs out of the basement two at a time. I had given up finding her and was starting to walk toward my car when I heard a honk behind me.

Leaning out of an SUV, Jenny was smiling. "Hey, girl. You need a ride home?"

I didn't. My car was only a few blocks away. If I rode with her, I'd have to take the bus back tomorrow before work. The buses were always late, and every time I took one I seemed to attract all the strangest people. The last time I was on a bus, I was sandwiched between a woman taking aggressive bites out of an apple and a man with a parrot on each shoulder. After every bite, the woman whispered the name "Ricky." The man with the parrots told me I was pretty but he was married.

"Yeah," I said, "a ride would be nice."

WE ENDED UP AT A DINER across the street from my car. Jenny had taken one look at the flashing OPEN and BURGERS signs and turned to me. "We have to stop."

"So—I'm going to tell you what my dad always used to say to me at diners," Jenny said once we were seated. "Don't look at the menu."

I dropped the menu, frowned. "Why not?"

"Because, whatever you want, it's probably on the menu.

Diners are pretty much all the same," she said. "Don't let the menu influence you, just conjure an image of your deepest desire and then ask for it."

"Your dad sounds like a cool guy."

"He is. How about yours?"

"Dead."

The waiter came by, reeking of weed and burnt bacon. Jenny handed him her menu and ordered a patty melt, fries, and a big side of ranch. "Big, China-big." I was in a breakfast mood, but not a meat mood, asked for eggs over easy and hash browns to soak up the yolk with.

"See? You didn't need a menu to know you wanted that."

Silence except for the frying of the grill and the occasional fork and knife scraping against plate. An elderly couple at the table next to us eating pancakes and not talking or looking at each other. A table of college-aged guys too enthusiastic about everything to have had anything less than a six-pack each. The guys cheered and pumped their fists in the air when the waiter refilled each of their waters. "Hey," Jenny said suddenly, grabbing both my hands in hers. "I'm really sorry about your dad."

"Oh." I looked down at our hands. "It's okay. I don't really want to talk about it."

She let go of them and nodded. "Okay, what do you want to talk about?"

It was an awkward question even though it shouldn't have been. I realized that directness wasn't a quality I was used to, that the conversations I had were often dictated by others and made me feel nervous, like I was trying to transport a handful of sand from location A to location B without losing a single grain. Conversations full of questions that were looking for very specific answers, leaving no room for any bit of thought or meaning. Existing on conversations like this was much like eating grilled chicken and steamed vegetables for every meal—doable, but dull. What did I want to talk about? So much.

Last week, I learned that raccoons were actually clean creatures. I was leaving Dad's shed at around 4:45 a.m. to crawl back into bed before Billy woke up when I saw a raccoon hunched over the cat's water bowl, meticulously scrubbing his paws as if he couldn't stand the thought of sullying the taste of two-day-old garbage spaghetti with dirt. He was washing harder than I did before my shift started.

No one knew I was an avid basketball fan. It wasn't that it was some big sort of secret, I just never had anyone to talk to about it. Dad had been a tight end for a semester in college and thought all sports where you weren't pounded into the ground were pussy shit. Billy was the type of athlete that thought nothing of sports after he de-cleated, Mom liked admiring the player's bodies but didn't care about strategy, who won or lost, all my old high school friends thought sports were low-brow. Tim Duncan was a badass motherfucker and I just wanted to say that out loud to someone.

I had been thinking constantly about han, a feeling that had been killing generation upon generation of Korean people. According to Mom, han was born in the gut and rose to the chest. Every injustice, every instant of helplessness, when the only reply to a situation was a mumbled

"Fuck this," all of it noted by an invisible scorekeeper in your heart. Han was a sickness of the soul, an acceptance of having a life that would be filled with sorrow and resentment and knowing that deep down, despite this acceptance, despite cold and hard facts that proved life was long and full of undeserved miseries, "hope" was still a word that carried warmth and meaning. Despite themselves, Koreans were not believers, but feelers—they pictured the light at the end of the tunnel and fantasized about how lovely that first touch of sun would feel against their skin, about all they could do in wide-open spaces.

I wondered if a more complex language like Korean had a singular word to describe the feeling of getting off a long shift of a physically demanding job and finding that, for at least half an hour after, everything, every last thing, was too beautiful to bear.

Jenny asked the question so simply—"Okay, what do you want to talk about?"—and I nearly reached across the table and grabbed her hands back, whispered thanks against each of her knuckles. I was about to ask her opinion on lakes and oceans—which did she prefer, contained and musty, or vast and salty?—when she suddenly sat up straight, eyes wide. "So—what did you think of that meeting today? Hold nothing back."

"Oh," I said. "I don't know, it was fine."

"Come on, you can do better than that."

"Okay," I said. "It was hard to sit through. And I don't mean that it was too long or that the seats were uncomfortable. It just hurt to be there, you know? Every time someone finished speaking, I wanted someone to hug me and then, immediately, I felt bad for being selfish. There didn't seem to be a right thing to say."

"It's the clapping that gets me, the forced support," Jenny said. "I just want someone to finish talking and instead of clapping, say, 'Wow, Patricia. That really fucking sucks.'"

I laughed. "I liked what you said in the meeting."

After a woman who was trying to decide the proper way to tell her husband she didn't want to name their future daughter after his dead mother, Jenny told the room about her hometown of Bismarck and how the sky looked different there, the flatness of the land allowed you to see more of it than in a place like Los Angeles, where buildings covered every square inch. The speed of things was slower there, people didn't walk places, but strolled. If someone in front of you in line at the supermarket was taking over a minute to fish out that last penny they needed from the depths of their bag, you wouldn't yell or ask for a manager, you just smiled and said, "Take your time." If you knew their name, and you probably did, you might offer them a penny of your own and tell them not to worry, there would be a next time and they could help you out then. Cheap gas, diner sandwiches slathered in mayo, multiple lakes a short drive away—there was no better day than picking up a grilled cheese and fries to go, eating them by the lake as you read your book, hopping off the dock for a swim when you got too hot. When you got home from the lake, damp and satisfied, one of your neighbors would probably be hosting a BBQ for someone's birthday, a husband's promotion, just because it was a day that ended in "y."

"Bismarck sounds like a nice place," I said. "I wish I grew up somewhere like there."

The waiter dropped off our food. What sounded good to me less than fifteen minutes ago now seemed disgusting. I shouldn't have gotten the eggs over easy, they looked too soft and runny, like the chicken who laid them barely had time to say goodbye. The hash browns glistened where I wanted them to be crispy. I forced down a few bites to be polite. Jenny finished half her sandwich and all of her fries before she spoke again. "I didn't grow up in Bismarck."

"But you said in the meeting?"

"Yeah," she said. "That was a lie."

I sucked on my fork. The metallic taste was soothing. "Where did you grow up, then?"

"Actually, not far from here. I went to high school around the corner. My first kiss was on the bridge over the 110 Freeway."

I pushed away the image of her kissing some faceless boy from my mind. "Why wouldn't you say that, then? Have you ever even lived in North Dakota?"

"I have. Of course I have. I went to college at NDSU and then lived in Bismarck after Adam was born."

Jenny with water dripping off her skin, her wet fingertips darkening pages of thick books, being kind in grocery store lines—this had to be real. "I just don't understand why you wouldn't say that, then. What's the point of lying? Why go to the meetings at all? Did you ever even have grilled-cheese lake days?"

She looked miserable, stopped eating, and began pulling the top of her sandwich off, tearing it into little pieces.

"Hey," I said, "I didn't mean to attack you or make you feel bad."

"It's not you." Jenny grabbed my hands again and this time didn't let go. I felt warmth and calluses. I wondered how she got them, what actions she'd committed so repeatedly that there was physical proof of them on her palms. "I don't know why I told everyone I was from North Dakota.

"When I was eighteen, I only applied to colleges in weird, faraway places. I ended up choosing NDSU. My mom and dad thought I did it to make them furious and maybe I did a little, maybe I was tired of being a smiling size-two who never broke curfew and was described by all her teachers as 'quiet, serious, a dream come true.' Mostly, I felt small every day and blamed the city, thought maybe if I went somewhere unlike anywhere I knew I could be fixed and new and like I'd always wanted to be."

"So you went to North Dakota."

"I went to North Dakota!" She let go of my hands and shoved a couple of torn bread pieces into her mouth. "I was so charmed at first. Los Angeles sounded so exotic to all my classmates, and at parties people were always refilling my glass and asking me endless questions about my opinion on this, that, whatever. The school's mascot was a bison, a big shaggy, horned creature. There was a statue of one on campus that looked so powerful, its body leaning into motion, front hoof forward. I liked reading by it, especially in the fall. I looked cute in a scarf and beanie."

"What happened?"

"What do you mean?"

"You said 'at first.'"

She paused, smiled. "You really listen to every word I say." I knew then that all the moments that followed would be in service to that one. I would be scratching my nose, brushing my hair, double-knotting my sneakers, driving to work, talking to Mom, Billy, Darryl, whatever hungry soul opened the door, standing in the shower scrubbing sweat, grease, whatever got stuck to me through the day off my skin, and I would ask myself—what are all the ways to make Jenny Hauser smile?

"So—what happened?"

Her hands were out of bread to tear. She clasped them together, tightly. "Nothing crazy or dramatic, just what always seemed to happen: I got bored. Everything I loved about North Dakota felt tired by the end of my sopho-more year. As I lay in bed every night it felt like an invis-ible hippo was sitting on my chest, and I couldn't help but think: I am wasting my life.

"One of the guys I was sleeping with was a city kid like me, but from New York. He talked constantly about the city and would earnestly call it 'the best place in the world.' It got me thinking that maybe it wasn't the city that had been killing me, but the wrong city. So I moved to New York that summer and never went back to school."

"I've always wanted to go to New York," I said. "My dad lived there for a little and played in a band. I listened to one of their records and they weren't very good, but I liked the idea of them playing in dark, smoky bars."

"I wasn't in New York long. Met a guy and moved to Miami. Then on my own again, headed to Austin, then D.C. when I thought I wanted to be in politics, Portland,

San Francisco, Las Vegas, Flagstaff, a brief month in Dublin, then back to New York City, Bismarck, and now here, Los Angeles again."

So many landscapes to picture her in. Her ponytail riding the subway, pushing through bodies and bodies on crowded sidewalks, surrounded by buildings so high she'd have to tip her head backward to see the tops of them. Her ponytail on a beach, salt and sunshine soaked into it. Among dark suits and conservative ties with the Washington Monument looming behind her. Hiking through forests in a haze of mist. Fruity colorful drinks with chiseled tan men. Casinos. Desert nights. More drinks, more men, but Guinness now, burly, red-faced men. Same skyscrapers, more bodies. Bismarck, a place I still didn't have a clear picture of. And now Los Angeles, her in front of me, mere feet away—I could reach across the table and grab that ponytail between my fingers if I wanted to.

"Why not just say that, then? That's all so much more interesting."

"Listing all those places doesn't make me feel worldly or fascinating or anything close. I like the idea of me being some doe-eyed Midwestern girl moving to the big city for the first time more than the reality. Because the reality is, I've been to so many places and not a single one has saved me. And I need Los Angeles to save me. I need this place to work this time."

I realized then that for her even to be sitting across from me she would've had to find someone to watch Adam. Whether a babysitter, a friend, her faceless husband, she called in favors or pulled out her wallet to go to the meeting in the church she talked so much shit about. I watched her fiddle with the edges of the menu, flip pages back and forth, mumble something about dessert—should we get some?—and thought about how easy it would've been for Jenny just to stay home if a small part of her didn't hope that the meetings weren't bullshit, that one day she would emerge from the church basement and onto the street, blinking rapidly, her eyes adjusting to the brighter, more beautiful world of a healthy, well-adjusted person, all of it unlocked for her by a circle of women.

I waved the waiter over. "Can we get a bowl of ice cream? We're going to be here for a while."

The waiter walked away, Jenny had that smile again, and I hoped she was thinking, yes, Los Angeles would work this time.

JENNY DROPPED ME OFF a couple houses down. The Freemans' front yard was cleaner, never a bag of garbage on their curb. "See you soon," she said before she reached across me and opened my door.

I watched her taillights until they turned the corner and let those words swell up inside me and carry me to my front door, up the stairs, and away from Mom's and Billy's worried faces and simultaneous sentences—"Where have you been?" "Do you know what time it is?" "We were so scared"—onto my bed, where I flopped, shoes still on. Billy crawled next to me soon after and I only distantly felt myself saying, "I'm sorry, I should've called. I lost track of time. It won't happen again, I swear." His arms curled around me and even those, in all their muscled solidity, felt barely there.

"See you soon"—no day attached to it, because why? She was a part of my life now, I was a part of hers. When you were a part of someone's life, you saw them, you didn't have to say a day of the week, you knew you'd see them. "Soon"—it was a beautiful word.

For the first night in a while, I didn't go to Dad's shed. I slept, dreamless.

7

THE LAST TIME I thought about a girl so intensely, I was sixteen and failing U.S. history.

There were a lot of reasons I was failing—lack of interest, the teacher had wandering eyes and a lisp, it was the class right before lunch and I was always tired and hungry, lack of interest—but the main one sat in front of me and her name was Becky Rivas.

On the third day of class, she had searched frantically through her bag, zipping and unzipping pockets, until she turned around and said five of the few words she would ever speak to me—"Can I borrow a pen?"

I had only the pen I was holding, a shitty blue Bic I used when I wanted to draw cats and dogs running across my legs. She was fully turned around in her seat, her eyes on me alone. It'd made me shiver, being stared at so closely. I gave my pen to her and she smiled, said the last four words she would ever speak to me—"Thank you so much."

I spent the rest of the class staring at the back of her

head, counting and naming the individual strands of her hair. When she leaned back and stretched, the ends of her hair would brush against my desk, hypnotize me with their sway. She would gather all of it between her hands, like she was going to tie a ponytail, then release it. I noticed she had three moles on the back of her neck, and I began writing haikus about them in my head. I wouldn't have taken notes even if I'd had a pen to do so.

The next month passed like this. The minute she sat down in front of me, I'd stare at the back of her head and try to work up the courage to tap her shoulder, say "Hey." It was the best I could come up with. I could never understand how people were able to start conversations out of thin air and keep them moving and breathing. Mostly, I waited for her to turn around and ask me for a pen again. She never did. My grade in the class continued to plummet.

One day, she went through the same nervous routine of rooting through her backpack. I sat up straighter, the hairs on my neck prickled, I was already reaching into my bag to pull out the many pens I now carried.

She didn't ask me, though, didn't even turn around. She turned to her left and asked Scottie Tsuji for a pen, and I stopped staring at the back of her head. Scottie had cornrows and thought it was hilarious to draw dicks on whiteboards when teachers weren't looking, which it was a little, but not as often as he did it. If she could ask Scott Tsuji for a pen, we were never going to be anything. I ended up passing U.S. history, got a C+.

This thing with Jenny was different.

Becky I only thought about passingly, mostly in the

hour before class. Jenny I thought about minute by minute. I began aching for Wednesdays and Thursdays.

It was impossible to deny the thing wasn't at least a
little sexual. I was masturbating every morning in the
shower again and, unlike the past weeks, I was able to
orgasm. Now my mind had something concrete to focus
on—baggy stained shirts, jeans that sagged sadly, crinkled
eyes, a ponytail that I wanted to wrap around my fist, pull
against my face, rub over my eyes, ears, nose, mouth, see if
it had the power to improve my senses, what did pepperoni and pickles taste like on her tongue, I often pictured
us standing close but not touching, just saying "Hey" back
and forth, her breath meaty and sour. I did my best not to
think about any of this on the nights Billy and I fucked.

When Wednesdays finally came, I wouldn't finish in the
shower. I'd get in and out as quickly as I could and put on
my uniform polo and jeans I'd made sure to wash the day
before, kiss Billy and Mom on the cheek, wish them a good
day, the best day. At Eddie's, I'd chug Hawaiian Punch, the
only drink we had without caffeine, to keep myself busy.
At 3:00 p.m., my body would be humming and my teeth
and tongue would be red. I'd go to the bathroom and pull
out the toothbrush I'd started to bring with me, scrub until
the red of the juice and the blood from my gums swirled in
the sink with the Crest foam. When I went back out, Darryl would often tell me that that woman had called, asked
for me. Even if he didn't, I'd know that she was calling
soon, that I'd be ready.

I never really remembered the drives over. I'd park
across the street and walk to her door in a sort of trance.

My first knock would be aggressive, the two after shy, then the painful seconds until the lock clicked open. If I'd wanted to write haikus about Becky's moles, I needed to write epics about Jenny's collarbones.

She'd never take the pizza right away. There were always things she had to tell me, details from our days apart— the egg she'd fried for breakfast the day before, which had been a double yolk, a good omen; a TV sitcom that she hated but couldn't stop watching; gray hairs she'd plucked; Adam's fights with his teacher; three plastic bags full of soccer trophies on the side of the road all with the name "Charlie Wilson," and how she spent the rest of the day wondering who this Charlie was and if it was him or his parents that put them there, why that day was the day that they were unable to spend another second with his childhood achievements shining on shelves. I hoped he wasn't dead. Yesterday, she'd been driving around when she saw a ninety-nine-cent store that called to her, went inside expecting just to wander the aisles, but immediately saw a bin filled with rainbow pinwheels that made her think of the fields of giant windmills she'd seen as a kid from the back seat of her parents' car on a trip to Palm Springs, wind turbine farms, how majestic they were, what a lovely trip it had been, her parents wearing sunglasses and lying around the hotel pool while she played in the water, splashing, churning her arms like those giant windmills, she bought the whole bin of rainbow pinwheels and stuck them in her front yard, see? I swallowed up every morsel she gave me.

After the stories ran out and I felt the box cooling in my hands, she'd give me cash and make me promise to be at the meeting on Thursday, always the same words when she closed the door behind her—"Take care, Pizza Girl."

I'd drive back to Eddie's and turn over the new details she'd given me in my mind. Sometimes I couldn't wait, I'd lock myself in the bathroom the minute I arrived and touch myself—us eating eggs off the same plate, my fingers weaving through her ponytail searching for gray, in a pool together, our arms moving in unison, water splashing left and right—other times, I wouldn't do anything. I'd go back to work and just enjoy those images, the idea of us together. If Peter noticed I'd been gone for too long, he'd take away my break. I never cared.

ONE MORNING, I sat on the toilet and sobbed to a Powerade commercial.

Billy and Mom had both gone off to work and I was alone in the house, sitting on the toilet, unable to shit. I wasn't experiencing morning sickness or swelling in my ankles, I wasn't needing to piss every time I took a sip of water, but I was lucky if I could shit even once a day.

Shitting was one of my simplest life pleasures. Before I was pregnant, each of my mornings would start off with me stumbling to the bathroom, plopping on the toilet with the lights off, and having one quick shit before my eyes were even fully open. It had been a little over a week without this routine and I was slowly going insane. That morning, I'd been determined to have my morning shit, no matter how long it took. I sat myself on the toilet and brought Billy's laptop with me. I was trying to watch Kevin

Garnett highlights, something that always calmed me, when an ad came up before the video.

A kid shooting hoops in a backyard with a net made from a milk crate, the backboard a piece of ripped cardboard. Another kid kicking a soccer ball alone in a field, a large bale of hay her goalie. The third kid just throwing a baseball against his bedroom wall, catching it, throwing it, catching it, over and over and over. A deep voice booms, "A mouse is drowning in a bowl of cream." The kid shooting hoops pushed to the ground as he walks to class, his ball flies out from under his arm and bounces down concrete steps. "Most mice would just give up." The soccer girl sitting on the sidelines watching a group of boys play a game without her. The baseball kid with his hands over his ears and his eyes closed as the yelling of his parents bleeds through the walls of his room. "But not this mouse." The first kid gets up off the ground and rushes down the steps to retrieve his ball. The girl stands up and hops into the game without asking. The third kid's eyes snap open and his fingers wrap around the baseball and squeeze until his knuckles turn white. "This mouse had fight. And, eventually, all that fighting churned that cream into butter." The basketball boy practicing relentlessly on his milk-crate hoop transforms into the leading scorer in the NBA. The soccer girl into the forward that kicked the winning goal for Team USA at the Olympics. The third, the star shortstop for the New York Yankees. They stand together, in a line, a powerful trio. "And that mouse simply climbed out."

The screen fades to black, and bold white letters flash across—"We're all just a kid from somewhere—Powerade."

Commercials were manipulative, I said to myself, a kind of evil, even the nice ones. The message didn't matter, they were all essentially saying the same thing. They spent thousands of dollars on actors and writers to make a script, produce thirty or so seconds of content to tug on your heartstrings so, in turn, you'd open your wallet to buy whatever product they were pushing. I knew all that, endlessly ranted about it to Billy when we were watching TV. So why did I spend the next thirty minutes watching that commercial on repeat, crying nonstop?

When my eyes finally remained dry through the entirety of the Powerade commercial, I clicked on others. Nike, Budweiser, McDonald's, Walmart, Toyota, Gap, Axe, Petco, Crate and Barrel, a small business that sold meat-flavored chewing gum—they all knew how to squeeze my heart, make my eyes blurry and wet. The minutes ticked by as I clicked and cried. I eventually stopped on a Tide commercial where a dad and daughter spend a day doing laundry together to surprise Mommy, to show her she doesn't have to do everything. She comes through the door and sees them folding crisp, clean shirts and pants on the couch and she bursts into tears. As they embrace, a Tide logo pops up in the corner of the screen.

By the end of that commercial, I had no tears left and decided, finally, it was time to get up and ready for work. Two hours had passed and I still hadn't taken a shit.

DARRYL HAD CALLED me earlier that day and asked me to please, pretty please, take Doug's shift that night.

"Why would I cover for Doug?"

"Because I need Sally to take my day shift tomorrow and she'll only do it if I find someone to take Doug's shift tonight. Did you know those two were dating? Personally, I think they both can do better."

"Okay, well, why can't you fill in for Doug?"

"I was already supposed to work tonight, but I got out of it, called in a favor with Kim."

"So, this is you calling in a favor with me?"

"Please? You know I wouldn't ask if it wasn't important. I'm putting on my good underwear and buying wine that doesn't come from a box."

"Special occasion?"

"Carl called and wants to come over tonight. If things go well, I don't want to have to be rushing out of bed and into work tomorrow, you know?"

"Who's Carl?"

"Damn, bitch. Do you not listen to anything I say about my life?"

"Oh, Carl, your cheating, lying ex-boyfriend."

"Do I pick up your shit and shove it in your face?"

I agreed, even though I hated night shifts. Pizza deliveries past nine weren't for dinner. Rarely families or couples sitting together at the dining-room table after a long day, cuddled into each other on the couch, no "tell me about your day" conversation. A lot of parties, or people in groups of three or more who had been smoking and drinking all night. They could be fun, would ask me to come in and chill for a little before I went back to work. Mostly, though, night shifts meant people alone in their houses, apartments, opening the door a crack and then only slightly wider when they saw it was me. They'd pay quickly, sometimes tell a hurried, stuttered story about how they didn't do this often, they were usually out with friends at this time of night, had cooked a healthy dinner hours ago, it had just been one of those days, you know?

Kim was also working at Eddie's that night. She wasn't bad, she kept to herself, cracked open one of her textbooks and read as she answered phones and jotted down orders. She was in her fourth year of community college, hoping to transfer next year to somewhere out of state. She told me once, in an uncharacteristic chatty mood, that she dreamed of becoming a doctor and moving to a third-world country to help decrease the infant-mortality rate. That night, she just said "'Sup?" when I walked through the door. I said "Hey" back. She returned to her organic chemistry book, I turned the volume up on my iPod. A song was playing that made me think of smashing things, large things, like watermelons, flat-screen TVs, wooden tables and chairs, jugs and jugs of milk.

A MAN WITH SIX CHIHUAHUAS standing in an unmoving row behind him, one with its tongue sticking out of its mouth. A woman in scrubs with a large stain on the pants that was either blood or coffee. Three girls with braces wearing their moms' clothing and heels, face masks, curlers in their hair, drying fingernails all the same shade of alligator green. A guy who took ten minutes of knocking before he answered the door, yelled at me that

I should've knocked louder, the pizza was probably cold now. A grandma type who tipped me a single dime. A small party, door answered by two dudes in sombreros. They offered me a can of PBR, icy cold, beautiful condensation, and I hesitated, but turned them down. A motel off the freeway, a dark parking lot that made me nervous, so I laced my keys between my knuckles, in 411 a guy in a robe that barely covered anything, a pair of crossed legs on the bed behind him. Several nondescript men and women in quiet apartments, every movement—the knocking, the lock clicking open, bills being pulled from wallets, change from pockets, cardboard shifting, that final slam, lock back in place—sounding unbearably loud.

It was an average night.

Rita and Louie Booker also called in. They were their usual selves, filling the doorway with their barely clothed bodies, hands gripping each other tightly, like neither of them would even be able to stand upright without the other. Rita had a cast on her left arm from a biking accident, a story she told hilariously. "And so that's the last time I ever try to do anything fucking healthy. The environment can suck a dick—I'm driving my F-150 to work again." They touched and cooed at my stomach, and it didn't bother me as much as when other people did it. I signed my name and a smiley face on Rita's cast.

I was driving back from their place, the radio was on low, the song just peaceful murmuring. One of the only bonuses of the night shift—the roads were empty. Empty roads in Los Angeles were a rarity. There were always people and they were always trying to get somewhere. Driving in traffic could send the kindest souls into yelling, spitting rage. I once saw an old woman who looked like she made the best apple pie, and remembered all her grandkids' birthdays, lean her head out the window of her minivan and spit at a Camaro that cut her off. "Your parents must be blind, or cousins, both!"

By midnight, everyone seemed to be where they needed to be. I could drive at speeds greater than ten mph, didn't have to slam on the brakes every other second, weaved from lane to lane just because I could. There was just a half-hour left in my shift and I was feeling okay. Then I looked down at my hands on the steering wheel.

Dad and I had the same hands. Small for our height, wide palms, thick knuckles, we both bit our nails until they bled. I'd spent many nights staying up late googling "plastic surgery for hands," going deep—not just page 1, 2, 3 results, clicking and scrolling, trying to keep my breathing clean and even, in out, in out, in out, 35, 36, 37, I made it once to page 78. One night, I came across an ad for a plastic surgeon in Beverly Hills who made a promise so grand and stupid it couldn't be real, but what if it was?—"Let Me Fix Your Pain for Good."

I sent him an e-mail—"Hi, please help me"—and he replied quick, a little too quick, paragraphs about rejuvenation procedures, cuts, and injections, promising to make me look young again. I never replied, didn't know how to tell him I was eighteen, my hands were still smooth, it wasn't about looking young. I had my father's hands, and in my dark, honest moments at 3:00 a.m. googling, I worried they weren't the only things of his that I had.

It could happen anytime, anyplace, instantly—typing a text, reading a book, cracking my knuckles, scratching my nose, turning on the lights, turning off the lights, grabbing a box off a high shelf, hanging with friends, sweating at parties, passing Mom an orange, holding Billy's face, working, so much at work—I'd be happy, laughing, breathing, and then I'd look down at my hands and I'd be sure he had those moments too.

I felt it strongly in the car. Dad was always going for drives late at night. I stared hard at my hands, our hands, gripping the steering wheel. He didn't just go for drives late at night, he went for those drives in the very car I was sitting in. I nearly ran into a lamppost.

BEFORE I EVEN WENT to work that night, Mom made sure that my cell phone was fully charged. "No excuses, you call us when you're off." I had called her when my shift ended at 2:30 a.m., said a quick "I love you," to both her and Billy, and was driving home when I decided there was just one place I wanted to stop first.

No lights were on in Jenny's house. No lights were on in any house on the block, just streetlamps and porch lights. I parked in front of the house across from hers and watched, willing a room to light up, even a lamp to flicker. I didn't believe she was sleeping. I knew she must have trouble going to bed, like me. Those bags under her eyes. Her constantly rumpled and stained clothes. I could hear it in the way she talked, someone who had been awake and thinking for too long.

I only planned on stopping for a minute or two, possibly just driving by if I could get a good glimpse of her through the window. It wasn't until I got near-simultaneous texts from Billy and Mom—"Where are you?" "Did something happen?"—that I realized over fifteen minutes had passed. I put the key in the ignition and was about to turn the radio up when, like magic, fate, force of my own will, the kitchen light flipped on and, a beat later, Jenny walked into my view.

The kitchen windows were big and I could see her clearly from my car. She was wearing a baggy long-sleeve shirt and even baggier flannel pajama pants. She looked small and comfy. I watched as she walked slowly around the kitchen, touching the counter, cabinets, sink, the knobs on all the drawers. After her fifth lap, she stopped at the fridge and opened it, stood in its glow for a minute before she grabbed a carton of milk and started drinking straight from it. She chugged until milk started dribbling down the sides of her mouth. She wiped her mouth with her sleeve, and she started pulling things from the fridge—eggs, sticks of butter, onions, lemons, a head of broccoli, a handful of wilting asparagus, a pack of hot dogs, something that might have been raw chicken, another carton of milk, a tray with a sheet of foil over it, takeout boxes, lots of takeout boxes—everything, until it was splayed on the counter behind her.

I wondered what she was going to make, what she could create out of the mess in front of her. She just stared at everything for a moment, and then, one by one, started putting everything back in the fridge.

She took her time, putting things in different spots than they were before. I wanted to rap on the window, tell her that raw chicken needed to be stored on the bottom shelf of the fridge or the juices could drip down and coat everything in bacteria, but I also didn't want to interrupt her process. She looked calm. When she finished she took another two slow laps around the kitchen and then started taking everything out again. I could've watched her all night.

My phone lit up again and I knew it was time to go. I was okay now anyway, looking at my hands didn't make me sick. I'd seen her, and in four days it would be Wednesday and I would see her again.

I started driving home, rehearsing a story in my head to quiet Billy and Mom: Hey, I'm sorry I'm late, I left something really important behind at work and just couldn't bear to let it stay there overnight, and I was craving something salty and sweet, potato chips and Kit Kat bars, that damn song from that damn commercial was stuck in my head, but all the gas stations were closed, and then I hit a pothole and got a flat tire and I had to fix it myself, I didn't want to bother you guys.

BILLY'S BEST FRIEND at work was a large man in his forties who went by "Semi."

Semi had recently gotten engaged to a Nice Girl, a second-grade teacher he met after rear-ending her Prius with his Hummer on the highway. His insurance paid for the accident, and he paid for several meals and drinks before she agreed to be his girlfriend. She went by "Lisa" and was considerably younger and smaller than him. I'd met Semi twice and he liked to make jokes about Lisa involving balls and chains, ninety-nine problems, all of them bitches. Every time I got up, I could feel his eyes on my ass. On Sunday, Billy told me Semi was throwing a party that night, one last blowout before his life was over and he became a married man. I fake-yawned, told Billy I was a little tired, he could go to the party by himself.

"I don't have to go to this, you know," Billy said, his hand wrapped around the doorknob.

"You should." I kissed him on the cheek. "Enjoy yourself."

Billy left, promising not to drink since he was driving home, he would be back before midnight. Mom and I stood next to each other, staring at the shut door.

I realized this was the first night Mom and I had been alone together in months, maybe longer. In general, I didn't have a lot of memories of Mom without another person in them. Before Dad died, we were either with him because he was in a good mood or, more often, he was in a bad mood and we were separate—me alone in my room, headphones on, her alone, wherever, doing whatever it was she did in those moments.

She turned to me and reached out suddenly, grabbed an end of my hair. I flinched and felt bad that I flinched, tried to relax. "You have a lot of split ends," she said.

Soon, we were in the bathroom. I sat on the floor, my back against the bathtub rim, Mom crouching behind me in the tub with a pair of scissors. She grabbed my hair, seemingly at random, and snipped. I watched pieces of my hair fall away, dark and sharp against the pure-white porcelain.

"My hair also got dry when I was pregnant with you," she said. "It drove me crazy every time I looked in the mirror, seeing how limp and frizzy it was."

I hadn't noticed anything different about my hair. My mirror avoidance had been working. I never caught more than a glimpse of myself in storefront windows as I passed, or my fuzzy reflection on the shed TV before I turned it on. When I ate cereal, I used a plastic spoon, no chance of even seeing my nose reflected in the metal. It was impossible not to see the top of my head in the rearview mirror when I drove, but I made sure to look quickly when I had to, focusing only on the road behind me.

"When you're in the shower after you put in conditioner, you should get a wide-toothed comb and run it through your hair before you rinse. It helps strengthen your hair. I read that in some article."

"I don't use conditioner."

Mom stopped. "What? Why not?"

"I don't know. It makes showers longer, it feels gross in my hair, I don't know."

"You should always use conditioner."

I wanted to turn around, grab both her hands, thrust them in the air with mine, scissors up, and scream, Yes, yes, this is what I want! Teach me, please. Guide me, move me if I'm headed in the wrong direction. Tell me how to do things. There's so much I don't know. "Thanks." I kept still, stared right ahead. "I'll start doing that."

She cut a few more pieces and brushed off my shoulders. "There. All done."

I stood up and headed for the door, thinking it might be nice to sit on the couch, just the two of us, and watch TV together, something light and funny. I had always enjoyed hearing Mom laugh. She grabbed my arm and stopped me before I reached the door. "Wait, look in the mirror. See how much better you look."

Her grip was insistent and I couldn't explain, tell her that staring into mirrors left me feeling weak, my insides scooped out, I hated seeing my own eyes staring back at me. I let her pull me to the mirror, and when I no longer could avoid it, I looked up.

In the mothers' support-group meeting, several pregnant women had complained about the distortion of their bodies. They moaned about how they couldn't recognize themselves anymore, so much extra skin and fat, their faces puffy and foreign. One woman had gotten up from her seat and lifted up her shirt, grabbed a chunk of her side, and waved it at everyone, shouting, "This is not my body."

In the mirror I saw the same girl I'd always seen. Her face was slightly rounded and there were bags under her eyes that seemed darker and deeper than before, but everything else was the same. Same nose, ears, forehead, mouth, the chin Dad always said was from his side of the family, a strong chin that had been passed down for generations and proved I was destined for greatness. Those women talked about how terrible it was to feel like they'd lost themselves, that they felt unrecognizable. None of that sounded too bad to me, being someone new, looking in a mirror and not recognizing the person staring back at you.

"Much better," Mom said. She stood behind me; her chin was softer than mine, and she barely reached my shoulder. "I couldn't have asked for a more beautiful daughter."

Are there other things you would've asked for? If you had the chance, if there was a way to go back, to be that girl in the convenience store knowing everything you know now, would you still greet Dad with a smile? Would you still say yes when he asked you to share a forty with him out in the parking lot? Yes to Los Angeles? Yes to me? What would I be like if you could've asked for everything you would've wanted for me? Do I look like him? Do you miss him at night? What is it like sleeping in a bed without him in it?

There were also questions I had about how she felt about me. I was so mad at her, and mostly I wondered why wasn't she mad at me when I told her I was pregnant. Why did she cry tears of joy when I told her I was pregnant and not tell me that I was making a mistake, tell me I should've used a condom, and I was too young to be having a child? Did she think that I couldn't be anything but a mother? That I was too stupid, too dull, to have a life for myself without a lovely man like Billy to provide for me? What would she think of Jenny?

I kept my eyes on my reflection. "Mom, I don't feel good. I haven't felt good for a really long time."

She turned me around to face her, mercifully pulling me away from my reflection. "Oh, honey." She stroked my face. I leaned into her palm, her warmth. "Are you having stomach pains? Or just body aches in general? Pregnancy really is rough on the body."

"No, I'm fine. I mean—"

"Do you want some tea?" She moved her hands from my face to my stomach. "Dad used to make me tea at night during the pregnancy whenever I was feeling sick."

"Really?" I removed her hands from my stomach. "He did that?"

"Yup. He even bought me a bunch of different flavors so I wouldn't get bored with any of them. He'd bring me a steaming cup in bed and tell me to close my eyes, see if I could guess the flavor."

It was hard to picture this. Him putting water in a pot, boiling it, steeping a mug with Earl Grey, English Breakfast, chamomile. I couldn't even picture him in the checkout lane at the grocery store with anything other than Miller Lite and jelly beans. That man bringing tea to his pregnant wife wasn't the same as the one who once picked me up from school two hours late, with crushed Miller Lite cans and gum wrappers covering the floor of his car, the front of his gray gym shorts soaked in piss, shouting over and over, "Get in, we're going to Disneyland."

I thought about telling Mom this memory, reminding her of that other man.

"Or is it something else?" she asked. "What can I do?"

She would never be able to help me. Her loyalties would always lie with him, this dead man who showed her sides he never showed to me. "Tea actually sounds nice," I said.

She went downstairs to make me tea and I swept all my

little hairs out of the bathtub, dumped them in the toilet, but didn't flush, just watched them float and clump together. Downstairs, we finally sat on the couch and turned on the TV, to a sitcom that filled all the pauses with the reactions you were supposed to exhibit—laughter, gasps, "awws." She gave me a mug of tea and told me to close my eyes and guess. I peeked, saw the green-tea label, and burned my tongue on the first sip. Took another, burned it further, and said, "I taste ginger."

DAD AND I didn't end up at Disneyland that day.

"You're twelve and you've never been to Disneyland," Dad said, trying to buckle his seat belt, failing. I reached over and buckled it for him. "How is that possible? Remember when we googled all those pictures of Mickey and Minnie? But not Donald, you don't like Donald." He slammed his fists on the steering wheel and the car felt smaller, his smell filling every corner of it. "We live an hour away. This has to be fixed today."

"I'm thirteen," I said.

He started the car and pulled out of the school parking lot. I didn't think I'd ever been in a car with him when he was sober, so nothing about his driving was out of the ordinary—some swerving, lots of honking, mumbles under his breath about how no one in this city knew how to drive a goddamn car.

We'd been on the freeway heading south for about five minutes before he turned to me, his face pale, his eyes glassy, staring at me like I was hardly even there. "I need my bed." His foot was barely pressed on the accelerator and we cruised down to sixty-five, forty-five. . . . When the car hit thirty, the honks started being directed at us. I put my hands over his and steered us to the shoulder. I pulled him out of the car, struggled under his weight. His full body pressed against mine, and I knew my T-shirt would stink of whiskey and sweat for hours after. Once he was curled up in the back, I hopped into the driver's seat, flipped on the turn signal, and eased back into traffic— I'd been doing this since I was ten, his designated driver before I learned the times tables.

We didn't go to Disneyland, but on the way home, I saw a sign for a Burger King drive-thru. I ordered three Whoppers and four large fries, extra sides of ranch. When it was time to pay, I smiled at the lady in the window and she either didn't notice or didn't care how old I was. She accepted the damp bills I fished out of my father's shorts pockets, handed me my bags without looking at me.

I parked in front of the house and ate two of the burgers and a fistful of fries before I went inside, dropped the rest of the food on the kitchen table for Mom. I left the keys in the ignition and him snoring in the back seat. I hoped he would take the hint and in the morning I'd look out my window and both he and his car would be gone.

Billy came home from Semi's party at 11:59 p.m. I wondered if the party was boring or if he really just wanted to honor his word and be back before midnight. I lay in bed, listening to the front door open and close, his heavy footsteps on the stairs. He entered the room and I quickly shut my eyes, mimicked sleep breathing—slower, heavier, relieved of the burden of being awake and conscious. He crawled into bed next to me and wrapped his arms around my waist, buried himself in the space where shoulder became neck. Once I was sure he was asleep, his breathing so easily what I was trying to make mine, I got out of bed and tiptoed downstairs to Dad's shed.

I stayed longer than I should have, flipping back and forth between infomercials and a Discovery Channel special about butterflies, tossing Dad's foam football against the wall, catching and squeezing it between my hands so tight it disappeared beneath my fingers before I released and threw again. I opened a fourth beer around 5:00 a.m. The first sip of it, I knew I'd made a mistake. I drank the whole can, but made myself throw it up on the grass outside after. I washed my mouth out in the kitchen sink and splashed water on my face twice, thought about how I'd still never been to Disneyland.

I ran up the stairs, two at a time, and threw open the door to my room, shook Billy awake. "Billy, Billy, you need to wake up."

He woke immediately, shooting up straight in bed like he'd been waiting for this moment. "What's wrong? Is the baby okay? What can I do?"

"Nothing's wrong," I said, kissing the corner of his mouth. "I just wanted to tell you that once the baby's born we're taking him to Disneyland. Like, every year we're going to bring him at least once and take lots of pictures— physical proof, so he'll never forget."

8

WEDNESDAY CAME. I was in the last couple hours of my shift and Jenny still hadn't called in.

I kept glancing from the clock to the phone, hoping. Every time it rang, my heart twitched and started pounding—it's her, it's her, it's her—but then Darryl would hang up and scribble down an order, I'd peek over his shoulder, and there'd be every order except the one I wanted, the names all wrong.

"Dude, what gives?" Darryl asked.

"What do you mean?"

"Why are you on my ass? And you're jumpy. It's tiring me out."

Darryl had been in a bad mood the entire shift. He'd walked in that morning wearing sunglasses and mumbled a greeting, sat on the stool behind the register and filled up a soda cup halfway, pulled a new bottle of Bacardi out of his pocket and filled the other half with it. I figured it must've been about Carl. He'd taken the sunglasses off, but was still moping.

"Sorry," I said. "I'll try and back off."

I couldn't stop, though. The phone rang again a moment later and I was back out of my seat, looking over Darryl's shoulder. "Bitch, I swear, I'm going to slap you."

The orders rolled in, and at each stop I said a fuck-you in my head to the person I handed the pizza to. I shoved a box roughly into the hands of a guy with face tattoos, flowers in place of his left eyebrow, the name Madison in place of his right. He laughed and said, "Damn, girl. Who pissed in your Cheerios?" A woman whose glasses made her eyes huge and buglike told me that I clearly needed to get right with God, the dark cloud surrounding me would kill me.

I worried about Jenny. My mind twisted itself into tight pretzel-shapes as I wondered where she was, what had happened to her that was preventing her from calling, what were she and Adam eating without their Wednesday pizza?

My shift ended and Jenny still hadn't called. I was tempted to hang around Eddie's and wait to see if she would, but Darryl's bad mood had only worsened. He yelled at another delivery driver, who changed the station on the boom box. "What the fuck, Stan? It was just about to reach the chorus." I didn't want to see what Darryl would shout at me. I avoided him until my shift ended and was out the door at 7:00 p.m. on the dot.

There's nothing wrong with driving by her house, I told myself. I wouldn't stay long or get out of my car, I just wanted to make sure she was okay. Her car wasn't in the driveway, and my mind felt so tangled I was afraid what it would look like once I unraveled it, if the knots were even untie-able. I pictured her car at the bottom of a cliff, even though I didn't know where she would find a cliff in this area. Men with vacant eyes and a dead-end alleyway. Tripping on a sidewalk crack, her head slamming open onto the pavement, red ribbons of her brain leaking out. Who would be at her hospital bedside?

I was seeing Jenny's body floating in the Pacific Ocean when her car pulled into the driveway. The car had barely stopped when she opened her door and jumped out, ran to the passenger side, and dragged Adam out. They walked two steps together hand in hand before he stopped, pulled his hand from hers. He stomped his foot on the ground, yelled something I couldn't hear. It was the most emotion I'd seen out of him. Jenny bent down and tried to take his hands back in hers and he ripped them away again, crossed his arms. She looked panicked, agitated, mostly scared. They both started to cry.

I was out of my car and moving quickly toward them before Jenny could wipe the tears from her face. I'd never been much of a runner, had moved even less since I got pregnant. The short sprint to them left me winded, a pounding in the space below my lungs, above my stomach. I stood panting within touching, tear-wiping distance of her before I fully realized the decision I had made, the choice to insert myself when I could've easily started up my car and pulled away, or even slumped down in my seat and watched quietly over my dashboard.

We all stood frozen, an awkward triangle. Jenny blinked

twice, a tear dripped down her chin into her open mouth. She wiped her face with the back of her hand, which only succeeded in making her face wet and shiny, the moisture emphasizing every line on her forehead, cheeks, the dimple in her chin. She looked cartoonish, a drawing of a starving, cave-dwelling creature. Adam made no effort to stop crying or wipe his tears, just centered his big eyes on me and waited.

"You didn't order a pizza," I said. "I was worried something was wrong."

Jenny stiffened. "Nothing's wrong." There was a sharpness, a tone I had never heard her use before. It hurt having it directed at me, the edges of those two words cutting, making it hard for me to swallow. "Sorry," I said. "I'll go."

"Wait." She grabbed my wrist before I could turn. "I'm sorry. I'm not mad at you."

"It's okay," I said. Words were funny like that. One moment they could wound you, turn into bricks that would sink to the bottom of your stomach. The next moment those bricks were transforming into butterflies, eagles, pterodactyls, Frisbees, various flying objects rising to your chest and nesting in the spaces between your ribs. I smiled at her, relieved that we were all good. Her fingers felt warm around my wrist.

"I could use your help, actually." Her grip on my wrist tightened. She stopped and let go of me and I grabbed her wrist back, tried to send a message through eyes and touch: Ask me anything, I can help with anything. "Could you watch Adam for a bit? I won't be gone long. I just need—"

"No." Our gaze broke and we looked down low to see

PIZZA GIRL ▼ 109

Adam with his arms crossed, shaking his head. "I won't stay with her. You can't leave again."

Jenny crouched down to his level, pushed his hair back, and kissed his forehead. "I'm not leaving. I'll just be gone for a little while." She kissed his forehead twice more and it seemed almost like a routine, as if she knew every step she had to take in order to calm him down. I tried not to think about how many times she'd done this before, how many times she would do this again. Another forehead kiss. "You won't even notice I'm gone."

"I notice," he said.

I put my hand on Adam's shoulder, kept my eyes on Jenny. "I'll watch him. Go, do whatever you have to do."

My hand felt awkward on Adam's shoulder as Jenny thanked me, handed me the house key, and told me just to let him watch TV, there was money for takeout in the left-most kitchen drawer, the one with all the batteries. She gave him one last forehead kiss before she turned and got into her car, pulled out of the driveway without looking at us.

We watched her car disappear around the bend. I was thinking about how I didn't have Jenny's cell-phone number, didn't know how Adam liked his sandwiches, crust on or off. "So," he said, tugging on my sleeve until I looked away from the spot where Jenny's car had been and at him. He was no longer crying. "What do we do now?"

ADAM HAD THREE stuffed animals he was on speaking terms with—Mr. Fuzzmister, King Cotton Candy, and Eric.

I gestured to the rest of the stuffed animals that crowded his bed, were crammed on his shelves. "What about all these guys?" He shoved the chosen three into my arms. "They're not important."

He insisted on showing me every inch of the house. He gave anecdotes as he pointed out landmarks—"And this is the hallway where I tripped once. This is the wall I drew on and Mom yelled at me. I like the color green and I want to grow up and own a store that sells large plants in tiny pots." He delivered all of these stories flatly, without looking at me. I carried the stuffed animals and nodded at everything he said and tried to ask good questions: "What shade of green and what type of plants?"

We ended the tour sitting on the living-room carpet. He made me smell a section of the carpet, didn't tell me until my nose was buried deep in the fibers that he'd peed there once because his friend Stevie double-doggy-dared him. I jerked my head up and fell onto my back, and he laughed. I thought that maybe we were friends now, that I would become one of the stories he told as he showed new people around the house, someone he told Stevie about, would beg Jenny to let me come over and watch him. This is why Jenny trusted me to watch him, I thought. She knew that Adam and I would get along, that if we were birds we'd be flying in the same flock. I started laughing along with him, and then he stopped, stood up, and said, "Okay, I want to be alone now."

He walked out a sliding door that led to the backyard, closing it a little more than halfway, just open enough to let a light breeze in. I stayed lying down, turned my face toward the sliding door so the breeze hit my face. I felt something that looked and tasted like rejection, but was deeper, more acidic, and I wondered if this was the feeling that parents got when their children slipped from their grasp, their gaze, and went somewhere they could not, a place where their voices became static and their hands lay stupidly at their sides—what do you do when you know you can do nothing?

Helplessness, I said to myself. I said it again, out loud, in the empty living room. Uselessness, I said next, hoping someone would answer, knowing there was no one. Mr. Fuzzmister, King Cotton Candy, and Eric sat next to me, slumped, their hard black eyes blank. I heard thumping. I thought it was coming from my own chest and then realized how idiotic and dramatic that was. I lifted my head, the thumping kept coming, and I knew it was coming from outside, Adam's doing.

The thumping was rhythmic, almost soothing—THUMP, silence, THUMP, silence, THUMP. Sometimes the silence went on a little longer than the previous one, but without fail that THUMP returned. I got up and put the stuffed animals on the couch, linked their arms together. The thumping continued, and I walked to the sliding door, hesitated, unsure of what was a violation of Adam's aloneness; after a beat, I pushed the door open wider, stepped outside.

The backyard was small and mostly dirt. A stack of bright-green squares of grass rested in one corner. An empty pool in another, with sludge and a couple Hot Cheetos bags at the bottom. A barbecue collected dust in the third corner, a sale tag still hanging off it. In the fourth, Adam stood, throwing a baseball against the back wall of the house.

His throws weren't casual, the throws of someone just having some fun, working off daily boredom. His throws were hard and direct. His mind was not wandering, it was focused—each thought connected to his arm, passing through his fingertips, heaved along with the ball and smack against the wall. The ball would bounce back to him and he'd scoop it up cleanly, throw it again, all his strength and will being used to snuff out the next thought that dared flit across his vision. Sweat dripped off his forehead and into his eyes. He wiped away nothing, just blinked and shook his head sharply, like an animal furious at the weakness of his body, that it would distract him from the task that lay ahead.

"Hey," I said. "Do you have a glove? We can play catch?"

THUMP. "I don't want to play catch."

"How about we go inside?" I pulled out my phone, looked at the time, tried to close my ears off to the sound of ball meeting wall. It was starting to make my head hurt; each thump was echoed by a throb from my left temple. "Have you eaten dinner yet? We can order delivery, or I can pour us a couple huge bowls of cereal. Even I can't mess up cereal."

"You could pour too much milk in it."

"You could pour your own milk if that would make you feel better."

"I can barely reach the counter."

"We don't have to pour the milk into the bowls on the counter. I could put the bowls on a lower surface, the floor."

"You don't have to be here. This isn't the first time I've been home alone."

He said all this without stopping his throwing. I had the urge to stand in front of the spot he was hurling all his frustrations toward and wondered if this would be enough to stop him or if he would continue, baseballs being thrown against my body, bruises blooming like deadly flowers beneath my skin. I could picture that happening without flinching. I could also picture him there night after night, the only sounds the thumping and his breathing, the small muscles in his arm twitching, exhaustion hanging over him like a fog, determination clearing it away. This made my hands shake, the cold Panda Express I'd shoveled down for lunch threatening to come up in a heap of chunky brown panic. Where was Jenny and did she know about this? If she did, how could she be driving? How was she able to grip the steering wheel with her shaking hands? What did the back of her throat taste like?

There was a bucket of baseballs by the sliding glass door. I picked one up and walked back over to Adam, stood by his side. The wall he was throwing at was covered in scuff marks, scars from his nights alone. Most were centered in one spot, but there were a few marks that lay solitary, off target, up high, down low, wildly to the left. Accidents, or bursts of desire to change things up, do something unexpected? I wound up and threw the baseball as hard as I could, at an untouched section of the wall.

I'd never liked the feel of a baseball. The game itself I didn't mind. I went to lots of Billy's games, cheered, clapped until my hands stung when he struck someone out or sent a ball sailing over the fence. When I held a basketball, I felt magic. Footballs didn't make me tingle, but they made sense to me, there was a comforting solidity when I gripped their laces. Baseballs were too small and hard, throwing them released nothing inside of me, I quickly grew bored.

That night, I threw the baseball with fluidity and ease. Each time the ball left my fingertips, I was crouching down, aching to have it back in my hands. The first few throws, I just marveled at the comfort of having simple, achievable tasks, a light, warm jacket wrapped around me, throw, catch, repeat. Look at my body, look at what it can do— Then my phone started buzzing and ringing in my front jeans pocket.

I didn't have to pull my phone out to know who was on the other end. There were only two possibilities and I didn't want to talk to either of them.

The ball bounced back into my hands and I threw it a little harder; that jacket of calm slipped off my shoulders. Did they get home from work and sit in front of the clock? They must've been huddled together on the couch, waiting until the time on the DVD player told them that there was no reason why I shouldn't be home. Who decided who would call first? Billy? Mom? Did they flip a coin or did they fight over the opportunity, hungry stray dogs clawing each other over spoiled ham straight from the dumpster?

Did they know how grating my ringtone was, what vibration felt like against skin?

The phone kept ringing and the throws piled up and all my unvoiced questions and thoughts became as much a part of the ball as the cork in its center, the rubber casing, the layers of wool and leather, each of its lacings. It was weird that Billy called my mom "Mom." It broke my heart how Mom drank her coffee every morning, how she so carefully put her lips on the rim and drank deeply, like she was grateful for every sip. Dad would pour pepper over all his food, and now I was afraid to put a sprinkle of the stuff on anything, even though scrambled eggs looked weird without it. If food could change people, I didn't want my baby to eat anything. I wanted it to exist on air alone and take in deep gulps of it, power born from within, no outside sources.

I started to picture the world without me in it.

I saw Billy at USC around other blond, broad-shouldered boys, smiling, blending into a crowd, his hardest job deciding whether he was going to go to his next class or take a deep, long nap on the campus lawn. Mom quitting her job at Kmart, a house with only her inside, dates with men who acted their age and wore suits and had nice cologne slathered on their necks and wrists, woke up every morning before she did, their briefcases full of things of worth. Dad was dead, buried at a cemetery by the highway—this was how it was and how it would always be. I didn't have to think of the baby: if I didn't exist, neither did it. The lack of my existence eliminated the need to imagine it, to wonder how it would do in the world, to see it crawling, walking, stretching to its full height, doing and saying things that I would have no control over, and becoming a person I had no doubt I would continually fail to understand, despite shared DNA. I added nothing—I had no hopes, no real tangible dreams that would make any lasting impact. If I was gone, worst-case, some pizzas wouldn't be delivered on time, Jenny would have to find another pizza girl.

The phone stopped ringing and I felt hurt, like they had heard my thoughts and nodded in agreement: Good idea, please stop existing. I threw the ball and let it roll past me on the way back, pulled my phone out of my pocket, and threw it instead against the scratched white wall of Jenny's house.

I stood, breathing heavily, the pieces of the phone scattered among the dirt. I could probably put the phone back together; only the battery popped out, the screen a little cracked. I heard a cough and I turned, remembering Adam was next to me. He was finally no longer throwing. "Let's go inside," he said. "I'm ready for dinner."

ADAM INSISTED that I sit on the couch while he made dinner. It sounded like he was just banging pots and pans together, opening and closing cabinets at rapid speeds. I let him be, there were no cries or scream for help, no loud "Ow"s! I tried to turn on Jenny's giant flat-screen, but there were too many remotes and buttons with symbols that made no sense to me, so I just sat quietly on the couch, avoiding the clock and trying not to think about the pieces of my phone that were lying in the dirt out back.

Beyond the screen door, it was black. The blue summer light I had been standing in earlier had been extinguished—the sky wouldn't let me pretend it wasn't late. Images of Billy patting Mom's shoulder with one hand, assuring her it was all going to be okay, his other hand betraying his true feelings, scratching the side of his neck, a tic of nervous frustration. The lines of Mom's face. She looked every year of her age and more. Her hair already had streaks of gray. She could name all of them after me.

I got off the couch, began pacing the room. I kept my eyes down on my feet in front of me as I paced, like I wanted to make sure they would work. This helped. One foot in front of the other, another task I could accomplish. My breathing started coming out in easy gusts, and when I felt comfortable enough to look up, I took one step, stopped, and found myself facing a wall and a framed photo.

I knew that Jenny was married, that Adam wouldn't exist without a father, but he lingered in a distant part of my mind, a man-shaped figure whose face and features, the little quirks and details that made him a living, breathing person, unknown. I liked it that way, was relieved that Jenny never talked about him. Seeing his face staring back at me made me realize that, even if I didn't want to know him, I had been curious.

It was a nice family photo shot in a professional studio with a camera that captured every pore, each eyelash. He stood behind Jenny and Adam, his hands resting on their shoulders like large, napping seals. They were dressed in matching white button-downs and jeans. It wasn't that Jenny's husband wasn't handsome—square jaw, no signs of balding, thick brown hair that parted smoothly to the left, eyes a shade of blue that made you think of warm ocean water, waves that didn't pound into you, didn't even crest, just sort of flowed into you and lifted you off the sand for a moment before gently placing you back down—he smiled without showing his teeth.

Jenny and Adam had wide, open-mouth smiles, their faces glowing, like there was nowhere else they'd rather be. Jenny's husband's face did not look like that. I stared at his lips, stretched into a halfhearted "u," like the photographer told him, "Look happy, now!" and that was the best he could muster. I wanted to reach into the photo and pry open his lips, grab the collar of his shirt, shake him, and yell, "Show some damn teeth!" That smile was not the smile of a man who had a son he could play catch with. This man saw his son's quietness and assumed something was wrong with him, didn't see that even while his son wasn't talking, he was watching, listening, trying to understand this world that continually flipped on him. One minute upright and comfortable, the next on his back, aching and confused. This man came home and pecked his eager, waiting wife on the cheek, went to sit in his armchair and lose himself in network television for hours after. In bed at night, he slept on the left side, she on the right, back to back. He should've been running through the door and pulling her into his arms, kissing her full-on, a little tongue, until his lungs and heart were ready to burst. When they went to bed, his arms should've been wrapped around her, no space between them. With a kid and a wife like that, this man's face should've been in a constant, toothy smile.

I STOOD STARING at the photo until Adam came into the room holding a plate of untoasted bread, cold beef and broccoli, a whole red apple, the sticker still on it, a Twinkie in the wrapper. "Every food group," he said. He could've put anything in front of me and I would've been touched.

We sat on the couch and he turned on the TV, using three different remotes, as I took a bite of the apple, poked the soggy broccoli with my finger, tore the bread into little pieces. Jenny's TV had more channels than I had ever seen and each one he clicked was available, not like in my house, when I clicked a cool-looking channel and a screen popped up saying I too could watch *Robot Turtle Race Wars*, for just $9.95 extra per month. Adam clicked through each one. We never spent more than a minute on each station.

"Do you have a favorite channel?" I asked.

"Not really," he said.

He flipped through more channels—a man jumping out of a helicopter, animated penguins singing a song about the importance of flossing, a woman about to either fuck a guy or murder him, Oprah Winfrey Network—and I kept staring back at that photo, looking away again.

"What's your dad like?" I asked.

Adam's channel flipping didn't lose its steam—old ladies racing down Route 66 on Harleys, a killer whale that washed up on the shore in Malibu still breathing, weight-loss frozen yogurt, a channel for either stoners or newborn babies, lots of flying colorful shapes and acoustic guitar–heavy music. "He's fine."

I heard his pain. "Fine," a word you used when you stubbed your toe and people asked you if you were okay and you didn't want to sound like a little bitch. When your mom gave you Cheerios after you asked for Froot Loops. Something you said to people who asked about your day and you didn't know them well enough to give them a real answer. Never a word used when talking about anything of value. "Where is he now?"

"At work. He has an office in this big building downtown. There's a fish tank behind his desk and he let me name every single fish in it."

"What're the names of the fish?"

"I can't remember. I only went to his office once."

"My dad was an asshole too. He died a little over a year ago."

Adam put the TV on mute, stopped clicking channels. "I'm sorry."

"You don't have to be sorry. He didn't die sad. He died stupid." I grabbed the remote from him, put the volume back on. "An old lady found him by the railroad while she was out walking her Rottweiler. The sun had just come up. He had been dead for hours." I turned the volume up a little louder. "Finally, he downed more booze than his body could handle. Like, seriously, don't be sad. It wasn't a surprise. For as long as I can remember, he was drunk. I don't think I ever really talked to him truly sober—he'd sit at the breakfast table pouring whiskey into his cornflakes."

On-screen, a group of children played in a field. Wildflowers swayed in the breeze, birds sang, the children laughed and called each other dickheads. I could feel something bad was going to happen to them and I didn't want to know what. I changed the station to one that showed handsome men and women running through obstacle courses in bathing suits. "There was one weird thing, though," I said. "The old lady said he was holding something tight, with both hands. A little toy police car. I spent weeks thinking about that police car, wondering why he had it and what he was planning to do with it. At times, I stupidly thought he saw it lying on the sidewalk somewhere and picked it up for me. When I was younger, I loved toy cars, and he would drive me to this big hill by the park and we'd watch my Hot Wheels cruise down. He would run to the bottom and grab every one, run back up so I could do it again. Maybe he saw that toy car and remembered that time and was feeling sentimental." I grabbed a piece of bread and swallowed it without chewing. "But then I remember who he was and I know he probably just saw a shiny thing on the sidewalk after he'd taken a swig and tripped, picked it up as an afterthought."

It was quiet for a moment, just the sounds of cheers from the TV as a woman with a six-pack and thighs wide enough to have their own ZIP code swung from rope to rope over a pit of mud. I wondered if Jenny had beer in the fridge. "I remember one of the fish's names," Adam said. "It was a blue fish with a long face and a frowny mouth."

"What was its name?"

"Joe."

"Why Joe?"

"There's a boy named Joe in my class who always flicks pencils at my back. Sometimes he spits in my pudding at lunch."

"This fish reminded you of him?"

"No, I just wanted to have a Joe that I liked."

The woman fell into the pit of mud and the crowd cheered even louder. "Do you want to keep flipping through channels?" I asked.

Adam took the remote from me. "Sure."

MY FINGERS ran through his hair over and over.

Adam was rapidly flipping through channels when, suddenly, he stopped and I said, "Is this a good channel? Do you like eighties workout videos?" and he just mumbled a "No," yawned, and lay down, rested his head in my lap.

I'd sat stiffly, unsure of what to do. I looked around, like there would be someone standing there to help me and move this child from my lap. For the first time, I wondered if Jenny was actually coming back soon or if I'd spend days, weeks here, throwing baseballs against walls and eating cold Chinese takeout and Twinkies.

Adam turned over so his face was toward me, and he looked so different when he was asleep—younger, more vulnerable—and it felt like the most natural thing in the world just to reach out and brush his hair off his forehead.

I kept brushing, as if my touch granted a layer of protection. He was so small, and this simple fact made me ache in a place deep enough inside me that I wasn't sure how to claw it out without mangling other parts of me in the process. When the ache began to affect my breathing, I scooped him into my arms and carried him upstairs to his room. Each step, I marveled at how little he weighed. I'd carried bags of flour at Eddie's that weighed more than him. I tucked Adam into his bed and arranged his stuffed animals in a line around him, bodyguards.

I walked out of his room and couldn't help but turn to my left and stare at the closed door at the end of the hall. Jenny's room. During Adam's tour earlier, he had merely pointed to it, saying he wasn't allowed in there, Mom spent a lot of time in there with the door closed. I hesitated for only a moment before I pushed it open.

The room was bare and I could see her clearly in there—lying on her bed, on top of the covers, hands crossed over her chest, eyes wide open and watching the shadows on the ceiling move. A laundry basket was in one corner and it was overflowing. I picked up one of the shirts poking out, a baggy long-sleeve she would be swimming in. I knew it was hers because of the tiny holes on the collar. The night I'd watched her, she chewed on the collar of her shirt while she rearranged the fridge. I brought the collar to my mouth and bit down. I chewed and sucked and tasted cloth and sweat, her sweat. It made me shiver, thinking about how her mouth had been in the same place as mine.

An engine's rumble and a car door opening and closing. I dropped the shirt and went to the window. For a moment, I worried that the man from the photo was home, but then I saw Jenny's ponytail swaying in the glow of the garage light. I took one more long suck and dropped the shirt back in the laundry basket.

I WAS WAITING right at the front door when she came in. She said, "Oh," when she saw me, like she forgot I would be there.

"He's in bed and we ate and watched TV," I said. Images of Adam and the baseball. "He's a good kid."

She softened. "He really is." There was a pause. "Do you drink whiskey?"

I thought at first she was calling me out and was relieved when she quickly laughed, shook her head. "That was stupid of me. You're pregnant. Of course you don't."

I stared at a point just above her head. "Yeah."

"Would you be okay watching me drink some?"

Back on Jenny's couch, TV off this time. She drank straight from the bottle, a brand I'd only ever seen on the high shelves of the liquor store. Every time she lifted her arm to drink, her shoulder brushed against mine.

"You must think I'm the worst mom."

"I don't think that."

"Well, I do." She took a long pull. "Ask me where I was tonight."

"Where were you tonight?"

"Drove around for a bit, wound up at the movies."

I could feel her waiting for me to say something, waiting for me to judge her, and it wasn't that I wasn't angry. Picturing her in a dark air-conditioned room, popcorn on one side, Coke on the other, made anger bubble up inside me. I felt it stinging the back of my throat, thinking about her sitting comfortably while Adam and I sweated and threw. But then I looked at her next to me—the way she was gripping the bottle, how she stared down into it, like she was hoping if she stared long and hard enough the solution to her problems would appear in the honey-brown liquid—and the bubbling stopped and melted into a tenderness, hot and thick, and I mostly just wanted to be in that theater with her, hear her laugh at the funny parts. "What movie did you see?" I asked.

She choked on the drink she was taking, coughing whiskey all over her shirt. I watched a few drops dribble out the sides of her mouth. "That's what you have to ask me? That's what you gathered from that statement?"

"Is there something else you want me to ask you?"

"I don't know, what about 'How do you sleep at night?,' 'When exactly did you become such a selfish bitch?,' or, better yet, 'What type of mother leaves her child with a complete stranger for hours?'"

The bubbling anger in my chest started up again, more intense this time. "A stranger." I said it one more time—"A stranger"—and the bubbling turned painful. "Is that all you think of me?"

"Fuck. No. Come on, that's not what I meant. I was shitting on me, not you. You're the best." She scooted closer to me and took my hand in hers and I smelled perfume, something tropical, whiskey, and I marveled again at how quickly she could quiet everything—no bubbling, no mess in my head, just my hand and hers, she said I was the best.

"Did I ever tell you what I wanted to be when I grew up?"

"No." I sat up straighter, squeezed her hand. "Tell me."

"I wanted to be a farmer by day and a rock star by night."

I laughed. "What does that even mean?"

"I liked cows and pigs and roosters and I wanted to play an electric guitar and be loved by millions." She was smiling, and I felt as warm as if I had been drinking whiskey too.

"That's awesome."

"Well, it is and it isn't. That was the last time I had a serious idea about what I wanted to be when I grew up." She wasn't smiling anymore, was back to looking at the bottle in her hands. "And I didn't even try that hard to make any of it happen. The closest I ever got to a farm was through the window of a car on road trips up to San Francisco to see my aunt Frannie. I just liked how wide and green the fields were and how peaceful the cows looked munching on their grass. I took three guitar lessons and quit because it didn't come naturally to me and I liked playing soccer better. There were lots of cute boys that played soccer."

"You were just a kid."

"Exactly! The last time I truly thought about my future and the mark I wanted to leave, I was eight years old. How pathetic is that? That's how old Adam is, you know."

"I didn't know that." He seemed both older and younger than that, and I didn't know which was sadder.

"Yup, eight years old." It was quiet for a moment, and then she was gripping my hand so hard I nearly cried out in pain. Her eyes were wide and brimming with tears that I was sure would burn me if they dropped onto my skin. "Every day, I am so afraid for him."

I wanted to pull my hands from hers, but her eyes wouldn't let me.

"The other day," she said, "I was shouting at my husband for leaving all the towels wet after showering, and then he came up to me and said, 'Mom, one day I'm going to invent a towel that dries in less than ten seconds.'" She took a drink and swallowed without making a face. "I mean, what the fuck? Ten seconds? He's so sweet and bold, he doesn't even pick a realistic timeline, skips minutes, goes straight to seconds. How's he going to feel when he realizes that those ideas will only ever live in his head? My head's a mess. Everywhere I go, I seem to find a way to trap myself. Most days, I can ignore it, but like anything you leave open and forgotten, it begins to rot. There are just too many thoughts, memories. I can't look at anything and not think of something else."

Jenny let go of my hand. There were white half-moons on my palm from her grip. "You don't get it yet, but you will. Soon, you'll have your own beautiful boy or girl who will look at you with their perfect little face and you'll feel love and hope and, mostly, you'll feel the weight of everything that's ever happened to you and everything that will ever happen to them and you'll want to run."

The half-moons on my palm were fading and I dug my own nails into them, tried to get them to stay a little while longer.

I COULDN'T STOP LOOKING at her hands. They held the bottle's neck so tight her knuckles turned white. Just when I thought the bottle might break, her hands would fall limp. The air in the room was thick and sour.

Our words weren't helping, falling out of our mouths and mixing terribly with the stink of booze, our sweat and breath. "Okay," I said. "There are probably lots of little plots of land you could get for cheap."

"What?"

"Like, for farming. There are still states that have tons of land and everybody eats corn, potatoes, strawberries, whatever else you grow in fields. It's not too late to learn guitar. My neighbors have this old pit bull, Chulupa, who used to run and jump and slobber over anyone that came within a few feet of her. Now, after lots of training and liver treats, they say, 'Hey, Chulupa, hey,' and she'll stop what she's doing and sit straight up."

Jenny didn't say anything. I continued: "Adam could totally invent towels that dry in ten seconds. My—my friend was going to go to a big college and learn how to make video games. I bet there's a school where Adam could learn about, uh, drying technology."

"Did you just compare me to an old pit bull?"

"I'm sorry. I guess I did."

"It's okay. I like dogs."

A buzzing sound started out of nowhere. I jumped, felt myself start to shake until I remembered that my phone was still in pieces. Jenny reached into her front jeans pocket and pulled out her phone, looked at the name on the screen, and slipped it back inside. She took a drink, and before she could even put the bottle back in her lap, my lips were on hers.

I'm sorry he leaves you here, traps you here alone in this house. I have phone calls I don't want to take too. There's a place I used to go when I felt lonely and small—not age- or body-wise small, I'm five ten in sneakers, I'm never actually small. But like when you're in a people-packed space and there's not a single face that looks at you for longer than a second—it's not invisibility, it's worse, they see you, they just have already decided in that second that there's nothing about you that's worth knowing, that kind of small. I liked sitting on the curb of the 7-Eleven parking lot. I'd get a Slurpee and sit a little left of the door so I could see all the people going in, but only their legs. A store across that street sold lamps, and it was always so, so bright.

Seconds passed without Jenny kissing me back. Seconds of she hates me, she doesn't feel my thoughts. A second more and her lips were pressing against mine, even harder, and I wanted to take her to 7-Eleven.

I'll get the cherry Slurpee, you get the Coke, we'll sip and kiss and it'll be fruity soda perfection. Bask in that lamp-store glow. You are beautiful and I will never make you cry, you will pick up every phone call from me on the first ring.

There was a fluttering in my stomach. At first, I thought it was just me and her—the softness of her lips, her hips melting into my hands—but then the fluttering was more insistent, something beyond me.

I stopped, put one hand against her cheek, took the other and pulled her hand from my neck, and placed it on top of my stomach. "Do you feel that?" I asked.

Kicking. It grew stronger with each breath I took. "Holy shit," I said. "Do you feel that?"

Her eyes focused on my stomach. Billy had been determined to be there for the baby's first kicks, was always talking to my stomach, reciting facts he knew—redworm composting is the key to a healthy garden; cigarette lighters were invented before matches; like fingerprints, every tongue print is different—but the baby had never responded before. Jenny's touch made the kicking grow stronger, thuds from the inside that shook me.

9

"BE CAREFUL."

The woman standing in front of me had long knotted hair, a bandage over her left eye, was wearing a T-shirt that claimed there was no place like Omaha. I wondered if she was a psychic, if the bandage was to protect her all-seeing eye. She took the pizza box from me and said it again: "Be careful."

My palms tingled and I wondered what she saw for me, what else she would reveal to me, what the fuck I should be careful of. There was so much I was desperate to know, but all I could really think to ask her about was what type of car I would drive one day, when I would be out of the Festiva.

"What—" I began, but she cut me off and said, "Your shoes are untied. Be careful." And then she handed me the money for the pizza, with a shitty tip, and shut the door so abruptly she nearly hit me in the face.

The rest of my shift crawled by. The details of the people I delivered to, forgotten nearly the moment their doors closed behind them. I was floating, not the peaceful kind, the kind people describe when their happiness is so strong that it propels them off the ground and pushes them lightly forward, no work required from their feet. I did not feel peaceful—I was off the ground and flailing, trying to find something solid to hold on to, something to keep me steady. It had been over a week since I'd kissed Jenny and not a word from her since.

I drove from address to address, barely there as I delivered. One house, I even forgot to take the money, was halfway back to my car before a guy ran out and grabbed my arm, making me jump. "Whoa, relax," he said. "I think you'll need this." He placed the money in my palm and closed my hand around it with his, like he didn't trust I could do it without his help.

Something was wrong. I sat in Eddie's and waited as the minutes ticked by and my shift dwindled to a close. I didn't think I would be able to stop myself from driving to her place and checking on her—How are you, Are you okay, Can you close your eyes without seeing our kiss?—until the phone rang, I stood up straighter, and then Darryl turned to me and said, "Hey, your man called and told me to remind you about your mom's birthday party tonight."

Billy and Mom hadn't spoken to me since the night at Jenny's house. It was lucky Jenny's phone rang again that night, causing her to remove her hand quickly from my stomach and scoot a foot away from me on the couch—I could've sat there all night. She looked at the number, put it back in her pocket, but when she looked up the moment was over. "I think you need to leave," she said. At the front door, she just gave me a quick double shoulder squeeze and told me to drive carefully, it was late. "How late?" I asked. "After midnight," she said. She shut the door before I could say anything else or kiss her again.

As I drove home, I'd imagined a wide, flat green field. At the edge of the field, a hill, and on the top of that hill, a house. The house was small and wooden and cozy, a fireplace inside with a roaring fire. Jenny was sitting in front of it, playing the guitar, and Adam was sitting in a large leather armchair, reading thick textbooks about things I'd never be able to understand. I liked the idea of the three of us taking long walks across the field when the sun was just starting to set.

I got home that night and opened the door to see Billy and Mom sleeping against each other on the couch. His head was back and drool was coming out the sides of his mouth. Her arms were crossed around her midsection. I wondered when the last time they got off the couch was. I clapped my hands together twice, loudly. They woke slowly, then abruptly—rubbing the sleep from their eyes, stretching, and, after seeing me standing before them, widening their eyes and leaping up from the couch. Before they could say anything, I clapped again. I didn't know why I was clapping, but it felt good and it got them both to shut up. "You guys," I said, "are driving me fucking insane."

We hadn't spoken since. When I woke up in the mornings, Billy would already be gone; Mom would leave me a breakfast plate on the table, then go to her room and play music loudly, to let me know she was home and ignoring me. When my shift ended the next Wednesday, I got into my car and drove past Jenny's street. I still hadn't fixed my phone, and my front jeans pocket felt empty, but good.

Mom's birthday party was at her favorite restaurant, a small Korean place that had Christmas lights up year-round. Her guest list consisted of me, Billy, and Nancy, an old Korean woman who waxed Mom's mustache and threaded her eyebrows once a month and also took bets on college football. There was a balloon tied to each of our chairs, and three wrapped gifts. One of the gifts was from me. I had no idea what it was.

Nancy was chatty, filled the space. "I have this great idea on how to revolutionize hot-dog buns."

Billy cleared his throat, politely asked, "What's the idea, Nancy?"

She smiled, took a dramatic pause. "As you obviously know, hot-dog buns are widely inefficient." We didn't know this. "Well, think about every time you eat a hot dog," she said. "There's always way too much bread left over at the ends when the meat is finished," she said. "Plus, sometimes the top and bottom separate, leaving you struggling to eat your hot dog in a classy way."

"I mean, if you're eating a hot dog, you're really not thinking much about classiness, are you?" I asked. I looked around the table for support from Billy and Mom. They refused to make eye contact with me.

Nancy ignored me too and plowed on. "So—my idea is to make a hot-dog bun that is more like a taco shell. Not in terms of texture, but the same shape."

"Sounds like a pita," I said.

"I also invented the washer-dryer, you know." Nancy waved down the waitress for more tea. "Well, I didn't actually—then we would be eating at a nicer restaurant—but I had the idea independently when I was a young girl, before I even knew that a washer-dryer already existed."

Nancy left before the food came, claimed she had another engagement to go to. "My son just bought a new house—very stylish, many bedrooms, a patio—and is having people over. He needs me there to help set the table and choose the right wine." She kissed Mom on both cheeks. "You'll like my gift. It's a shower radio. I'll see you in a week for your appointment."

We watched her walk out of the restaurant in silence. The food came and we ate intensely, eyes down on our plates, stuffing more food into our mouths before we finished chewing. When our plates were empty, I could feel the panic, the three of us unsure what to do. "I'm going to open my gifts," Mom said.

Mom opened the shower radio from Nancy, a Snuggie from Billy. "I know you get cold when you're watching *Jeopardy!* reruns late at night." Then Mom picked up my gift and looked at me for the first time that night. I wish that she would've looked angry, that her eyes would've been piercing and fiery, that she would have been directing all her years of disappointment at me. But her eyes were soft and full of warmth and forgiveness, she looked like she wanted to reach across the table and hold me against her. I reached for my water glass and drank from it even though it was empty.

Mom was thirty-seven tonight. For the first time, I thought about how she was closer to Jenny's age than my own. I tried picturing the two of them standing next to each other. Their differences went beyond the obvious—height and weight, hair and eye color, the way their faces changed and the lines that deepened when they smiled—Jenny was more of a person to me than Mom had ever been.

I thought about how Mom's first name was Choon-Hee, although, the minute she stepped off that plane and her feet first touched American soil, she told everyone to call her Kayla. I knew that those were still her names, but I'd never thought of her as anyone other than Mom. I couldn't imagine her talking the way Jenny did. To me, her vocabulary was limited to a small selection of words and phrases—Hi, Good morning, How was your day, Are you hungry, I can make you something, Your dad always loved, Good night, Sleep well, How is the baby—I couldn't imagine her with her hair long, tied back into a ponytail, creating shitty paintings, lying all day on a couch dipping Hot Cheetos into a tub of cream cheese. It must be true that, like Jenny, she had so much life ahead of her, so many things she could do. But I could only picture her going gray in that Kmart uniform. It made me ache to think of Billy and me moving out of the house one day; I couldn't imagine her bringing another man into her bed, a man who would only know her as Kayla, who'd whisper that name as he closed his eyes and pressed his lips against hers. I'd never seen her kiss Dad on any place other than the cheek and forehead when he'd passed out drunk on the couch.

Mom peeled open the wrapping paper of my gift. Underneath, there was a framed photo of her, Dad, and me, when I was just a baby. They looked young and beautiful and their smiles were wide and open-mouthed. They held me between them like I was the answer to all their problems. Mom stared at the photo and began tearing up, held the picture to her chest. "This is lovely. Where did you find this?"

Billy saved me. "She's been looking at a lot of your old photo albums. That's her favorite photo."

Mom cried quietly for a few more minutes, until her birthday apple pie was brought out by a waitress. Mom hated cake—frosting made her teeth hurt. As she blew out her candles, I made eye contact with Billy and mouthed, "Thank you." He nodded back, and his eyes were also soft and warm, and I couldn't stare back for more than a few seconds. I was too full to eat any pie.

ONCE A MONTH, we stayed late at Eddie's and held a competition for who could fold a hundred pizza boxes the fastest. The winner didn't actually win anything. Folding pizza boxes was part of our job, we just wanted to make it fun.

"Sixty-two," Darryl said. "Where are you at?"

"Fifty-five," I said.

"I'm at seventy-six," Willie shouted.

Darryl gave me a look and turned his shoulder an inch

away from Willie. "So—Carl and I are really done this time."

It was my turn to give Darryl a look. "No, no," he said, "I really mean it. I just can't take it anymore."

"What can't you take anymore?"

"Loving someone more than they love me."

We stopped talking and focused on the folding. I wasn't very good at folding quickly, but I secretly didn't mind this part of the job. "Oh," Darryl said, "did you hear about what happened with that couple you like?"

An image quickly popped into my head—Rita and Louie Booker standing in their doorway, barely clothed bodies, arms never not around each other. "The Bookers," I said. "What's up?"

"So my buddy Marv lives in the apartment next to them and apparently the husband—"

"Louie."

"He was beating the shit out of his wife."

"Rita."

"I guess he had a thing for punching her in the stomach, so that no one could see the bruises. Last night, the cops were called. The EMT said he was beating on her so hard that she started vomiting blood."

I was having trouble folding the box in front of me. My hands were too shaky. "That can't be true," I said.

"Afraid so. Marv looked out of his apartment and saw the wife being loaded into an ambulance, the husband being shoved into a police car." Darryl sighed, shook his head. "I really did like them. They were always polite over the phone."

"I liked them too."

I played back every time I had ever delivered to them in my head. I pushed my mind to re-create every last detail: What was the color of Rita's shirt, why did Louie scratch his nose like that, what did Rita mean when she opened the door, smiled, and asked me, "Hey, girl, how's it going?" Was she trying to send me a message, trying secretly to say, "Hey, girl, how's it going? Help me, I'm scared and I don't know what to do, I'm dying here, every day I'm dying, and I don't know what to do or who will save me, can you save me?" I remembered this one time delivering to them, about a month ago, and she complained of a sore back. The last time I saw her, there had been a cast on her left arm.

I stopped folding boxes and braced my hands on the table. I saw them kissing and laughing and loving each other in my head, and then I remembered that the beer in Dad's shed was nearly gone, five cans left.

"Hey, Willie," I said, "can you go up front and get me a big cup of Diet Coke? I'd go myself, but I'm really behind you guys on my boxes."

He frowned. "But if I leave I'll lose the contest."

"Willie, the contest isn't actually a real contest," Darryl snapped. "Like, we don't get anything if we win."

Willie walked out of the kitchen, head bowed.

"After work, I need you to come with me to a liquor store and buy me a couple cases of beer."

Darryl stopped folding too and stared at me. "I can't do that for you."

"Oh, okay."

Willie ran back in and practically threw a full cup of

Diet Coke at me. A little sloshed out and spilled onto my shoes. We didn't say anything to each other for the rest of the competition. It was silent until Willie yelled, "One hundred! Done!" and Darryl yelled back, "Shut the fuck up, Willie! No one cares!"

WILLIE'S CAR wouldn't start. Darryl and I played Rock, Paper, Scissors to decide who would stay and help him jump-start it.

Best two of three, he beat my paper with scissors, I rocked his scissors, but on the third round we kept picking the same thing—paper-paper, scissors-scissors, rock-rock, scissors-scissors. Willie stood in front of us, doing his best not to look completely pissed. After we tied for the fifth time, we sighed, shrugged, and both went to help Willie hook his Malibu up to my Festiva.

We got Willie's car to start and waved until his taillights turned the corner. We burst out laughing.

"He's right to hate us."

Darryl abruptly stopped laughing and put his hand on my shoulder. "Are you okay?"

"I'm fine." I shrugged a little, hoping he'd take the hint and move his hand away. It stayed. "Why are you asking me that?"

I expected an immediate answer—Darryl was so smooth, always had words on his tongue that he was ready to spit out, no matter what situation—but he just stood there, hand on my shoulder, opening his mouth and closing it. "I don't know," he said finally. "I'm just worried about you."

"You don't have to worry about me. That beer thing—I was just kidding."

"No. You weren't." Darryl moved his hand from my shoulder, shoved it into his pants pocket. "And it's not only the beer thing. You just seem like you haven't really been here lately."

"I'm here all the time. I've never missed a shift."

"I'm not talking about attendance. I'm just saying that even when you're here, even when you're doing something or talking, I feel like you're somewhere else. I can always hear you thinking. Not like your actual thoughts, but I can hear the strain of it. I don't even know what you do when you're not here. Like you didn't even tell me when you were pregnant, you just came back from lunch one day with an armful of pregnancy tests, and then, another day, you're asking me to cover your shift so you can go to the doctor. I guess I figure you must be lonely, and all I'm trying to say is, if you need someone to talk to, you can talk to me."

Darryl was staring down at the asphalt and leaning his weight from foot to foot, both his hands in his pants pockets. I didn't think I'd ever seen him so uncomfortable, and as I watched him rocking back and forth on his feet, sweating in his ugly Eddie's polo, I felt strongly that he was a good person. I knew so many good people. "Darryl," I said, "I'm fine. Don't worry about me, worry about you. Carl's going to call you again and you're going to answer, so you better prepare for that. Find a real friend to talk to about it, not just some girl you work with."

He tried not to look hurt, but I saw it, even if it was only for a second. I tried to communicate to him silently that it was better this way, he didn't want to sit across from me and hear everything that was swirling around in my head—even if he could hear the strain of me thinking, it didn't compare to the sound of my actual thoughts spoken, hanging in the air.

"Okay," Darryl said. "I'll see you whenever our next shift is."

I got into my car and he got into his. I waved as he pulled out. He didn't see.

RITA AND LOUIE BOOKER'S place was empty. I knocked on the door until my fist started to hurt and a guy in a pink robe poked his head out of the apartment next door and asked me to please fucking stop.

"Marv?"

"Dale. Now please go away."

I got back into my car and was headed home when I remembered it was Thursday. It was weird to go to Jenny's house. It wasn't weird to go to an open-to-the-public Current and Expecting Mothers meeting held at the local church.

She wasn't at the meeting. I tried to walk back up the basement stairs when I scanned all the heads and didn't see her ponytail among them. A very pregnant woman in a cutoff T-shirt that ended just above the swell of her belly smiled at me, her teeth yellow and crooked, the front one cracked; she put her hand on my shoulder and said, "Stay."

"Each chicken nugget has about fifty-nine calories in it.

Seventy-two calories per mozzarella stick. A whole PB and J has approximately three hundred and eight-five calories in it. I haven't done the math to see what a single bite is. I have to stop eating what my kids are eating."

"I'm having sex dreams about everyone, and I mean everyone. The other night I woke up sweaty and throbbing after dreaming the bagger at the grocery store had his head between my legs. I gotta tell my husband, right?"

"There's this bird that sits outside my window every morning and it won't stop chirping. I'm slowly going insane."

"Maybe you could put one of those bird feeders outside your window," I said.

Every head in the room swiveled to me. The woman who'd been talking was frowning, her nose wrinkled. "What?"

"Maybe the bird is chirping so much because it's hungry. I just thought maybe if you got a feeder it might help the noise."

The woman gave me a tight-lipped smile, then quickly turned away from me. "So this goddamn bird is waking me up at four a.m. every goddamn day. My shift at the diner ends at two a.m., it takes me twenty minutes to get home, then I have to slip my mom a twenty and some home fries for watching the kids, I have to brush my teeth and put lotion all over my body—trying not to look like a leather handbag one day—and my mattress is hard as a rock, it takes me at least another twenty to get to sleep. You all do the math—how much sleep am I getting each night?"

I didn't speak again for the rest of the meeting. Outside

the church, the night actually felt cool for once. No dark heat, a breeze too. A hand gripped my arm and I turned to see a young pregnant girl, the one I was almost 80 percent certain I'd gone to high school with.

"Hey," she said, "I have one of those bird feeders in my backyard. The birds really do like it. I saw a blue jay the other day."

She looked so young. She smiled and I noticed she had braces and I wondered what I looked like to her.

"Do you want to go grab a coffee? There's a diner not too far from here."

The rubber bands of her braces were a bright neon-green. I thought I remembered her from ceramics class, sitting in the back, chewing the ends of her hair when she thought no one was looking.

"I can't," I said. "I have to go home. Maybe next time."

10

ON FRIDAY, Jenny finally called.

I was sitting at an empty table making a giraffe out of straws with my iPod on, the volume a little higher than I was used to. When I got home the night before, Mom had been sitting at the kitchen table, all the lights off. I wouldn't have even known she was there if I hadn't gone to the kitchen and opened the fridge to take a chug of orange juice. The carton had barely touched my lips when I heard a voice behind me. "Hi."

I spilled orange juice down my polo. "Jesus, Mom. Why are you sitting in the dark? Did we run out of lightbulbs again?"

"Do you hate me?" she asked.

"Why would you think that?"

"It's hard not to think it with the way you've been acting. Please look me in the eye."

"I don't hate you."

"Then why are you always trying to leave?"

I turned on the lights and settled into the chair across from her. I tried to think of something to say, but failed. Mom got up after a while, I don't know how long. She just patted me on the back and told me to sleep well. I went to the shed and finished three of my last five beers.

Now Darryl had to pull my headphones off and yell into my ear to get me to hear him. "That woman wants her pizza."

I put together Jenny's pizza with joy. I found a rhythm as I cut the pickles, the perfect even sprinkling of them; when it came out of the oven I wanted to cry and have a slice for myself. The cooks gave me a big cup of water with ice.

The song on the drive over was one I would've normally skipped over. Slow, syrupy lyrics that coated your tongue, got stuck on your gums. I didn't mind it then, added lyrics of my own.

I walked up to her door, an extra bounce in my step. I felt like my life would've been different if I'd had this bounce all the time. I would've gone out for the school basketball team, straight A's wouldn't have been a problem, friends either, I would've been the loud one in the cafeteria. Before Billy and Becky Rivas, I'd had this intense kind of crush on this girl in my English class who never spoke unless called on, spent the whole time writing in her notebook, her long green hair protective curtains on both sides. Mr. Keener wasn't that interesting, his tests were the same multiple-choice ones he'd been using since the 1980s, answer keys up for sale—she couldn't have possibly been taking notes the whole time. I would've had no problem going up to her after class, putting my hand on her shoulder, asking to read her notebook, please. I always had to beg Mom and Dad for rides or promise near sainthood in order to borrow one of their cars—none of that, I would've happily walked everywhere, no matter how many miles away.

I heard the lock on her door click open. I ran a hand through my hair and gave the gum in my mouth one last strong chew, spit it onto the lawn. Jenny answered the door and I thought I might throw up.

Her ponytail was gone. If she'd tried to gather her remaining hair and tie it up, it would've formed a small, sad palm tree. Her new cut stopped a couple inches above her shoulders—not a mom bob, but also not her. I blinked a few times and wondered if she had looked into the mirror after the hairdresser was done, and been as devastated as I was now, her hands moving to the ends of her hair and mourning what she had lost. I tried to find positives— lightweight, quick drying after a shower, it could be fun to bang your head to loud music, watch the strands spring back and forth. But I could only see what had been, the long, flowing freedom that fell softly down her back, tied up by a yellow elastic hair-tie.

She stood there in front of me, smiling like nothing was wrong. "Your hair." I couldn't make any other words come out of my mouth.

"Do you like it?" She twirled like she was a doll or the young heroine in a movie, a quirky girl you just had to root for.

"Why did you do it?"

Her smile fell. "I don't know, I just wanted to. Why do I need a 'why'?"

"You don't, but there usually is one."

We stood there, so much space between us. This wasn't how I thought it would go. The door was supposed to open and she was going to look at me and I was going to look at her and we'd just look at each other and know it was all going to be okay. I didn't know that now. It wasn't just the haircut, as unsettling as it was to see her looking like someone she wasn't—there was more. The space between us felt deliberate, her eyes were flicking from my face to beyond me. I almost turned around to see what she could possibly be looking at. But I kept my eyes on her, wanted to reach and close the gap between us. I knew I would be okay if I could touch at least a part of her.

"I just wanted a change, is all," Jenny said. "And I figured, where we're moving, short hair might come in handy."

My palms itched, but I refused to scratch them. "Moving? What do you mean?"

"Oh, well, Jim is getting transferred to the company headquarters in Bakersfield. We're leaving early tomorrow."

"How is that possible? How can they just make you leave in one day?"

"Well, the house is owned by the company—they could relocate us whenever they want. But they haven't just given us a day to move. We've known."

"We." I tried not to get stuck on the word. "How long have you known?"

"A little over two weeks."

I couldn't stay standing any longer. The palm itch was

forgotten and it was now my knees that were causing me trouble—shaking, wobbling. The air up where I was standing seemed too thick, it was impossible to swallow. Jim— why was she saying his name now? I turned away from her and sat on her front steps. A little over two weeks—while we kissed, was she already miles away? The sides of the pizza box were dented by my grip.

I felt Jenny sit next to me on the steps, her hand hovering over my back. I was grateful when she didn't retreat, but laid her palm flat against the curve of my spine. "You can't leave," I said.

"I don't really have a choice here." Only one layer of fabric between her hand and my back. "Jim can't say no to this offer. It's a big opportunity for him."

That name, that damn name—Jim—its sound, short and hard, bitter on my tongue, sliding down my throat like a spiked eel. "What about you? What about Adam?"

She shrugged. "Jim says we'll like Bakersfield. And I bet Adam will be happy to leave. Maybe he'll find a better baseball team there."

I moved her hand from my back and cradled it on top of the pizza box. Dad used to read the lines of my palms and tell me stories about the things the different ones said about my future: "Wowee, that big line there means big money! You going to share any with your old man? I'd love a flat-screen!" I wondered which line on her palm had to do with me.

"But what about you?" I asked. "Do you want to go?"

"Well." She didn't say anything for a while. I looked away from her hand to her face and felt exactly the same as when I first saw her—an ache without a central point, equally spread in every blood-flowing part of me—I still wanted to run away with her to anywhere with sun and ocean.

"Sometimes," she said, "grown-ups have to do things they don't want to do. Unfortunately, I am a grown-up. I'm turning thirty-nine in December, you know?"

I'd had a feeling that she had a winter birthday. "You don't look thirty-nine."

She smiled. "Liar."

She was right. I was lying. I'd figured she was in her mid-forties. I smiled back. "Okay, I was lying."

As she laughed, she reached up to grab the end of her hair, but missed, not used to the new shorter length. She absently groped around her left breast before she realized, moved her hand up, and twirled a tiny piece around her index finger. "You can't leave," I said again.

She ripped a corner off the pizza box and asked me for a pen. I handed her an Eddie's pen and she started writing something on the cardboard. "This is my new address," she said. "Write me a letter, send me a picture of that baby of yours once it's born."

She helped me up. "Thanks for the pizza. Adam will be really happy to eat it one last time before we leave. Who knows if there will be a pizza girl in Bakersfield as lovely as you."

TOO MUCH MONEY shoved into my hands. I wanted to say something for her to remember me by, something for her to think about on the drive up to Bakersfield, as she unpacked her boxes in her new home, in her new bed later that night, back throbbing from bending and carrying, eyes fluttering shut with exhaustion, I wanted my words to wrap around her and protect her. All I could think of to say was "If you need help moving, my Festiva holds more than it looks like it could."

She laughed. "I think the movers can do the job just fine."

Before I could say anything else, even think to kiss her one last time, she closed the door, said softly, "Take care, Pizza Girl."

I COULDN'T FINISH MY SHIFT. The only thing that seemed possible for me to do was to go home and stand in the shower until my skin felt raw and pink and clean or the hot water ran out. I called Eddie's from a pay phone across the street, watched Darryl pick up.

"Are you sick?" Darryl asked. "Is it the baby?"

"I just can't. If Peter gives you shit, tell him I'll clean the bathrooms every day for the next month."

For the first time in I didn't know how long, I drove without the radio on. I also realized I was crying, because my vision went blurry, only clearing after I blinked rapidly a few times, saltiness dripping into my mouth. The Festiva made so much noise that I'd never heard before, over the music.

I parked crooked in the driveway. I didn't have the energy to fix it. Jenny was moving to Bakersfield and I just wanted to scour every inch of my body, the roughness of a loofah making me forget what it'd felt like when she put her hand against my back, how I wished for all five of her fingertips to become permanent islands on the fabric of my shirt.

Each stair to the bathroom was agony. The first step, I remembered going to the grocery store that first time and being stunned by the amount of pickle brands, not knowing which one Adam would prefer. The second step, I was inside Jenny's house, staring at her seven shitty paintings. The third, she handed me the painting of the turtle with a dented head and it was the most beautiful thing I'd ever seen. Fourth step, I tasted chicken and peanut butter, saw my reflection as I threw up into that blue, blue toilet water, could feel Billy's and Mom's warm breath on the back of my neck. Fifth step, Rita and Louie Booker, so madly in love. Sixth, my hands on the steering wheel, Dad's hands. Seventh, Adam throwing that baseball against the wall over and over and over. Eighth, Dr. Oldman and the ultrasound, his mountain-range daughters. Ninth, tenth, eleventh, twelfth, Jenny in her doorway, her ponytail still intact. When I reached the second-floor landing, I thought I might pass out.

I breathed deep and focused on just getting to my room, willed myself not to remember anything else. I pushed open the bedroom door and inside was Billy, standing in front of the mirror, both his hands wrapped around a gun.

II

BILLY AND I sat next to each other on the end of our bed, the gun and complete silence between us. I wanted to get up and turn on my stereo, but I worried that any sort of movement would break this fragile space we were existing in—the remaining time before we'd have to look at each other and acknowledge that there were things that we really had to talk about.

We'd stared at each other for a long moment, completely frozen. Me in the doorway, unable to cross the threshold, and Billy in front of the mirror with his back to me, my eyes on his reflection's, the gun witness to it all. He opened his mouth and I turned around and ran to the bathroom.

I didn't need to throw up, although I tried and dry-heaved into the toilet. Billy came in then and I thought he was going to help me, hold my hair back or kiss up and down my spine, and I was ready to push him off, maybe even hit him, but he just closed the door behind him and lay on the floor beside me. I heaved a few more times before I lay next to him and discovered that he had good instincts—the bathroom tile was cold and felt good on my exposed skin.

I was about to strip naked so every inch of me could feel the cool tile. Before I could, he asked me how I was feeling, how the baby was doing, could he get anything for us, maybe a glass of water, and I was mad all over again. I sat up and said, "Billy, what the fuck is going on?"

He looked at me like I'd slapped him. I staggered back to bed without turning back to him, pressed a pillow over my face. Images of pushing Billy into the soft sheets and whispering apologies into his ears and mouth for how I'd been acting, how I couldn't seem to say anything anymore that didn't come out like glass, a bottle being thrown against pavement, all its pieces jagged and uneven and scattering like roaches fleeing light.

After a while, I heard him get up and follow me. He brought a coffee mug of water with him and I took it wordlessly, drank it all in one clean gulp.

BILLY NEVER KNEW when the worries would start.

Sometimes he'd make it a few hours, he said, maybe into early evening. Other times they would hit him before he even left the house, as he was making breakfast, or stepping out of the shower. A particularly crushing set of worry hit him once as he was squeezing toothpaste, and he became so overwhelmed he put the brush down untouched. When he came home after work and saw the brush still sitting there, the toothpaste dull and crusty, the crushing feeling intensified. It was never a question of if the worries would hit, but when.

There were no limitations to the worries. Billy's brain, the thing that had done him so right in high school, was now working overtime to dissect every thought that flitted through his head, until he could barely take a step without having a minor panic attack.

Of course, every worry eventually circled back to the baby and me. Example: He'd be mowing lawns and sweating and he'd start worrying about global warming, which would lead him to thoughts about the melting of Arctic Ocean ice and the death of polar bears—my face starting to peek into the forefront of his thoughts, my growing bump. He would try and switch his thoughts to something more pleasant, like Popsicles, but then Popsicles would make him think again of sweating, of global warming—what if it eventually became so hot that every drop of water sprayed out of every sprinkler just evaporated and then, lawn by lawn, entire cities started drying out until there was no grass, just patches of dirt, and no job for Billy to do, no way for him to earn money, and if he didn't have any money, he couldn't buy Popsicles, and what type of childhood could someone have if they didn't know the taste of cold, artificial cherry, orange, grape? One of his favorite books he read as a kid featured a baby polar bear, and even if he was able to afford that book, how could he tell his son that all the polar bears in the world were dead?

Billy was at work one morning when he got stuck on a string of particularly toxic thoughts. He felt so on the verge of a breakdown that he found Semi at the water cooler—Semi, whom he considered to be a guiding hand, a big brother—and told him all of his Popsicle, polar-bear worries.

Semi pulled out a joint and offered it to him. Billy said he didn't smoke, and then Semi suggested that, well, if he didn't smoke, why not take one of Semi's extra guns? It sounded like what Billy was really worried about was his ability to provide for his kid and baby mama. Whenever Semi was a little stressed about money, he and his cousins would rob a convenience store or find some yuppie at an ATM to scare the shit out of. After work, Semi took Billy to his car and wrapped a handgun in a T-shirt, slipped it into Billy's backpack before he could say anything else.

The first few days, Billy couldn't even look at the gun. He kept it in his backpack and put it in the corner of his closet, bought a different backpack to take to work. He got through the days the same way he'd gotten through all the days before them—minute by minute, trying to keep his mind on the task ahead of him, sweating. Then, on the sixth day after being given the gun, he was home alone and lying in bed and thinking about pens, how approximately one hundred people a year died from chewing on their pen caps and choking. He began cataloguing everyday items that could pose a danger to his son, all the shit he'd have to throw away in our room before the due date. The sheets beneath him grew wet and he started wondering if it was possible to sweat to death. He vaguely remembered reading about a medieval sickness called the "sweating sickness," which killed people within twenty-four hours—what would happen to me and the baby if he was dead? Billy jumped out of bed and ran to the closet, zipped open his backpack, desperate, willing to try anything to get his brain to stop.

He didn't have to hold the gun long to know that he would never be able to rob anyone. No matter how desperate he got, it made him nauseous to imagine pointing the gun at another person, much less pull the trigger. An image that made him even more ill—his son visiting him in jail, pressing his hand against plexiglass.

But that day, Billy found something else that was helpful.

Holding the gun made him feel calm. The gun was sleek and black and heavier than he thought it would be, felt so solid in his hand. He stopped entertaining the idea that he would do anything with it and started just holding it and staring at himself in the mirror. The person looking back at him in the mirror was someone he trusted, a person that stood tall and didn't spend his waking hours in his mind, a man of action, a man that never started sentences with "Could I" or "Would I," because he knew in his heart that, yes, he could, and, yes, he would. This man was someone that didn't cry in the shower every morning or feel the need to pinch the inside of his thighs or dig his nails into his palms because he was so scared that he would never be able to make the love of his life and his unborn child happy.

WE WERE LYING down on the bed. When Billy started talking, he'd been facing me. I don't know who did it first or at what point, but by the time Billy stopped talking, we were both on our backs, side by side, not touching, eyes glued to the ceiling. It helped not to have to look at each other.

"Why didn't you tell me any of this?"

"Why are you home from work now? Your shift isn't over until 8:00 p.m."

"What does that have to do with anything?"

Billy sat up. I tried to avoid eye contact with him, but he wouldn't let me, hovered over me. "It has everything to do with everything—you never talk to me anymore, so how could I possibly feel comfortable talking about anything with you? What chance would I have of actually getting through to you?"

"What do you mean, you never have a chance to talk to me? We see each other all the time." I patted the bed. "We live together."

"Yeah, exactly. And that's about it." He was off the bed now, pacing, scratching the side of his neck, like he always did when he was nervous. "We see each other all the time, but we never talk. The little we do is about nothing; I mention the baby, our baby, and you turn to stone." Billy stopped pacing and looked away from me to a point above my head, a blank wall—my room had no decorations. "I'm so lonely."

He said it so softly, so genuinely, and for a moment, I remembered him on that first day we hung out—how rapidly he ate scoop after scoop of ice cream, the crumbs of the cone falling into his lap, the napkins he ripped in halves, quarters, flakes of paper snow, how everything he said made me want to rip my heart into halves, quarters, throw the tiny pieces on top of his napkins.

He looked back at me and then I was the one that wanted to look away. "Sometimes I'll stand in front of that mirror talking to myself. I'll tell myself stories about my day, or stories from my past, my future, things I dream about, that I can only see when I close my eyes. When I get tired of talking about myself, I'll pick up something to read out loud. Books, newspaper articles, receipts, ingredients on the backs of snack foods—did you know on Goldfish bags in addition to all the chemicals and shit, it says 'Made with smiles'?" Billy himself smiled for a second at that, but then seemed to remember who he was talking to. "Basically, I say everything that I should be saying to you."

It was impossible not to hear the anger in that last state-ment and impossible to ignore that that anger was because of me. Did he ever talk to his reflection about me? Was his voice this angry whenever he mentioned my name? I remembered that the other day I was sitting at the kitchen table and he asked me, "Do you want your eggs scrambled or sunny side up?" and I said, "Yeah, sure." I used all the hot water in the mornings, and he never said anything about the cold showers he would take after mine. I ignored so many of his phone calls, our text conversations were filled with long, lovely messages from him and short, choppy replies from me, if I even bothered to reply. He got me roses a few weeks back just because, roses that I never put in a vase, just let sit in their wrapping on the windowsill slowly wilting until they were brown and their petals had fallen in a dead heap on the floor. I never saw him clean them up. I just woke up one day and they were gone.

I couldn't stand looking at him anymore. I rolled off the

bed and sank down to the ground, on top of a pile of dirty clothes.

A few seconds later, Billy was in front of me, on his hands and knees. He grabbed my face between his hands. "Are we okay? I just want us to be okay."

I stared at Billy, the person I loved, the father of my baby. "We're not okay."

His hands slipped from my face, drifted down to the tops of my knees. "What does that mean?"

"Just that—we're not okay."

"You said that already. Can you say more?"

"I don't know what else to say. We're just not okay."

Billy's grip on my knees tightened. "Please stop fucking saying that."

"Let go of me."

He quickly stood up. "Okay, if we're not okay, you're the reason why."

"Fuck you."

"Fuck me? No, fuck you!" It looked like Billy was going to hit me, rage distorting his face as he brought both his fists up above his head. I closed my eyes and waited for them to come down against me. Nothing came. I opened my eyes and saw Billy back on the floor, crying into his fists.

"I love you," he said. "I love you so much and I'm so mad at you and I can't even tell you how mad I am at you. The other day I woke up and went into our bathroom and there was water all over the floor, you'd left the sink running all night. I went back into the room ready to fight about it, wanting to fight about it, but when I opened the door you were just sitting up in bed, looking out the window. I stood in the doorway for a full five minutes, and you didn't even turn your head." He looked up at me, tears dripping off his cheeks, and I wished he had hit me. "What do you do in the shed in the backyard every night?"

Hit me, I can't have this conversation, hit me, please, anything other than this. "I—I don't know what you're talking about."

"Do you think I'm stupid? Do you think I don't feel you get up in the middle of the night and come back hours later?" He was still crying and his voice was cracking. He had to stop in the middle of his sentence to wipe his runny nose on the sleeve of his shirt. "I haven't said anything and I haven't gone inside the shed because I believe in privacy and I know you're struggling, I know your dad dying has been hard on you—"

"It hasn't been hard on me."

"Why don't you talk to me anymore? We used to talk all the time. We would just lie in bed holding each other and telling the other every little detail about our day, stories from before we knew each other, everything we hoped we would do together. Do you remember that? I think about it all the time."

I did think about those days. Maybe not all the time, but I did think about them. I was hurt that he even had to ask, that he couldn't trust the beauty of those moments, that he didn't know that in those moments I had been so happy I was almost sad, knowing that those moments would end and I couldn't live forever in that bed with him. "I do remember," I said.

"I just miss you so much. I know you're going through a tough time, but so am I, I hate this. Have I done something to get us here?" He pushed himself up and crawled over to me, grabbed my hands again, but softer this time. "Tell me what I've done and I'll fix it."

"You haven't done anything."

I wiped the tears from his cheek, ran my thumb over his bottom lip, and kissed him. He kissed me back and he tasted so like him—a taste that wasn't describable, but made me think of comfort and how the roads smelled after it rained. I hoped before our kiss ended I could figure out how we could go back to before, to my bedroom when we had just met, and talking was as simple as opening our mouths and saying whatever thought popped into our minds, the words flowing out like Froot Loops from a never-ending box—colorful and sweet and so light that you could hold a whole handful without feeling like you were weighed down by anything.

WE DIDN'T TALK FURTHER, fell asleep before nine, before Mom was even home from her shift.

I actually did sleep, heavy and dreamless, but only for a few hours. I woke up at 1:32 a.m. soaked in sweat. I looked at Billy next to me and got out of bed as quietly as I could, pulled on my sweatshirt, and turned to leave, and Billy was awake and sitting up.

"Do you have to go?" he asked.

"Yes," I said.

12

THE NEXT NIGHT, at 12:21 a.m., I was driving to Bakersfield with Billy's gun in the passenger seat.

I'd planned none of it—I'd gone to my shift that afternoon and been called into Peter's office. He asked me if I liked how he'd decorated it. I said that I liked the wallpaper and he said that there was no reason I should know what his fucking wallpaper looks like, that if I ever left work in the middle of my shift without getting his permission, I would be fired. "You do not want to see this wallpaper ever again."

My shift felt purposeless knowing Jenny wouldn't call. Everyone I delivered to seemed nice, but I couldn't look at them without wondering what their lives were like when they closed the door behind me.

An old lady with hands so shaky she nearly dropped the pizza box—so many years she'd lived, how many people had she destroyed in her life?

A bearded man in a once-white T-shirt who I could

smell from the doorway—did he ever leave his apartment, did people call to check in on him?

A teenage girl with bangs that covered her left eye—be careful, keep those bangs long, hide yourself.

An apartment window with an absurd amount of cactuses in front of it. They grew so tall I couldn't see their ends past the top of the window. They were so dense that when I tried to look into the apartment in the thin spaces between them, I couldn't see anything. I rang the doorbell several times and no one answered. I stood, a warmish Hawaiian pizza in my hands, and wondered if a man or a woman owned those cactuses.

When my shift ended, I stopped at a liquor store. It was on my way home and I knew that I would need more than my last remaining beer that night. Even as I was stepping out of my car, standing in front of the liquor store, watching people go in, searching for a friendly face, I still wasn't visualizing Bakersfield and Jenny's arms, how they'd wrap around me when I pulled her from bed. I was just thinking about how impossible sleep would be that night, how long I would have to wait next to Billy before I could get up and go to Dad's shed, open one of the beers I was hoping to have bought.

The first guy I asked looked at me and shook his head in disgust, the next said he would do it if I gave him a handie in his car, the third just walked right past me. Finally, a girl a little older than me walked up. Her hair was in a loose ponytail, not as long as Jenny's old one, but she had that same kindness, warmth. She gave my stomach a long look, but agreed, took my cash, and went inside.

She came out a little while later with a thirty-rack of Miller and a small flask of Evan Williams.

"Thank you so much," I said. "My dad is having a bad day and—"

"Hey, it's okay. You don't have to give me some bullshit story." She handed me the beer and the whiskey. "I'm sure you've got your reasons."

She walked away and I stood there for a moment watching her ponytail swing behind her, the beer heavy and cool against my hands.

I made it through the rest of the day. Mom, Billy, and I ate dinner together. While they did dishes, I snuck the beer and whiskey from my car into the shed. After, we watched TV. I even made them laugh, told them a story about a guy I delivered to once who shoved Hot Wheels up his ass, how he told me he did it because it just felt so damn good when they were taken out. It felt normal and comfortable, and when Billy grabbed my right hand, Mom grabbed my left, I didn't even mind, squeezed both of their hands back.

In bed later, Billy and I were holding each other quietly. Sleep was tugging on my eyelids when Billy asked, "We're going to be good parents, right?" Through the dark I could see the panic in his eyes—this wasn't a rhetorical question. "Right?"

I closed my eyes tight. "Right."

Even as I was getting out of bed, walking downstairs, pulling my shoes on and double-knotting them tight, I had no idea that in an hour I would be speeding down the highway blasting rock ballads, a gun rattling to the bass in

the seat next to me. In the shed, I pulled out a beer, and
the fullness of the fridge made me relax, the Evan Williams bottle on top of it a beacon of hope.

I was halfway through my second beer when I pulled
out the piece of pizza-box cardboard that had Jenny's new
address written on it. She was already there, was just set-
tling into bed in a new strange place that she'd now call
"home," the word tasting weird on her tongue. I traced
my fingers over the cardboard, admired her handwriting,
some of the letters loopy and carefree, the "a"s and the
"o"s and the "c"s, others tight and cramped, those poor "t"s
and "l"s, unable to stretch and loosen and exist how they
were supposed to—this was not when I decided to go to
Bakersfield.

This was:

I remembered one of the last conversations I had
with Dad.

I'd been walking home from a party. My friend Alisha
offered me a ride, but the booze was making me feel alive,
and nothing felt more alive than walking home in that
easy Los Angeles night, the only music my breathing and
the neighborhood sounds.

I was five minutes away when I saw Dad walking from
the opposite direction. There was no way to avoid him—we
both needed to turn down the same street. He raised his
hand. "Hey, there. Looks like we had the same idea."

"No, I had an idea. You're just too drunk to drive. I bet
tomorrow we'll find your car in the middle of the park
again."

He laughed and we walked next to each other.

"I think the Dodgers have a real good chance to get to the World Series this year," he said.

"The Dodgers were eliminated from playoff contention two weeks ago," I said.

"Ah, right. That sounds right. They just rip our fucking hearts out every year, don't they?"

"Dad, why're you so fucked up all the time?"

I tripped. An uneven stretch of sidewalk and I was on the ground, the knee of my jeans ripped open, dirt and blood. He knelt down next to me, pulled a flask out of his pocket, poured some whiskey over my cut, and blotted it dry with the sleeve of his jacket. "This is how they did it back in the Old West, before doctors and peroxide."

I pushed his hand away. "Do you know how much you hurt Mom every day? Me? I don't even know what you actually smell like, you always smell like booze and sweat."

He plopped down on the sidewalk next to me. "You know, I try to quit every morning I get up. I lay in bed and I look up at the ceiling and I say, Hey, motherfucker, this is the day everything changes. Sometimes I make it days, weeks. I was sober the first year of your life, believe it or not." He took a swig from his flask. "But some days, I don't even make it an hour. I get out of bed, go downstairs, and I need to pour myself a drink. Because you know what I've learned, no matter how long I wait? That I will never be someone that is effortlessly good, it'll always be hard work for me, and I'm not that strong.

"I think some people are just born broken. I think about life as one big Laundromat and some people just have one little bag to do—it'll only take them a quick cycle to get through—but others, they have bags and bags of it, and it's just so much that it's overwhelming to even think about starting. Is there even enough laundry detergent to get everything clean?"

"People aren't born broken," I said.

"Well, if they're not, that's scarier. Because if I wasn't born broken I don't know when it happened. I can't look at any point in my life and say, 'Aha! This is the moment!'" He put the flask to his lips, paused. "Sometimes I think your mom and you would be happier if I just moved to an island in the middle of nowhere."

I took the flask from him, had another drink. "That's not true."

We sat there quietly for a while, looking out at the street in front of us, wondering when we could get up and start walking home.

I hadn't thought about that night in a while. I finished my beer and grabbed an armful more from the fridge, put the whiskey in my pants pocket, ran out of the shed. I had lied to Dad that night—Mom and I probably would've been better off if he'd just packed up all his shit one day and never come back—I thought that and I lied.

I put the beer in the Festiva and walked quietly back to my room, pulled Billy's backpack out of the closet, and put his gun in my other pants pocket. Dad may have sat back and given up, but I wasn't going to be like that. I wasn't born broken. I wasn't going to live alone on an island in the middle of nowhere.

▼

JENNY WAS LETTING THAT MAN, that Jim, tell her what she needed.

I knew she had to be awake right now, unable to stop her mind from twisting, no way to turn off that small part of her that still hungered for a life of her own making. The navigation said I was thirty minutes away from Jenny's house in Bakersfield. I pressed my foot harder on the pedal, ready to get to her house and tell her that it didn't have to be this way, not for either of us, I was there now and we had all the time in the world to figure out our laundry situation, which bag to start with and every drop of detergent needed. I reached for another beer, my hand brushing against Billy's gun in the process.

You needed to bring it, I told myself. You need to be able to protect yourself and Jenny. I'm sure she'll want to take Adam wherever we go. Jim may not handle it well. When he learns that his wife and his son are leaving him, he will probably yell, scream—animals that are backed into a corner do desperate things. You will not have to fire the gun, I told myself. But you have to be ready.

I STOPPED AT A GAS STATION just outside the city limits. The tank was still half full, but I liked the idea of me showing up at Jenny's to offer her a car with a full tank of gas, a car of possibilities. I bought a Coke from the attendant and then emptied it out in the bathroom sink until there was only a small layer of soda covering the bottom, poured the whiskey in. I was about to get into my car when a police cruiser pulled up to the pump next to me.

Two cops stepped out of it and began walking in my direction. I opened the driver-side door and reached over to the passenger seat, adjusted my hoodie, prayed that it was covering the whiskey, the beers, the gun.

The taller of the two, with a mustache I wondered if he'd had before he became a cop, stopped in front of me, looked at my belly before he looked at my face. Even my baggiest T-shirts were starting not to fit. "It's late," he said. "You should get home. Lots of sickos out right now."

"Yes, Officer," I said. "Of course."

I took a sip from the Coke can, got into the car, put the Coke between my thighs, and pulled out of the gas station, waving to both of them. A drop of sweat collected under my nose, but I couldn't take my hands off the wheel to wipe it. The cop had been standing close enough to me that he could've reached out and wiped any sweat from my face, close enough that he could've smelled whiskey on my breath. My foot twitched on the gas pedal. I was trying not to drive recklessly fast, not to drive suspiciously slow.

I kept my eye on the rearview, waiting for red and blue lights, and wondering why the fuck I couldn't have waited to take a drink until I was safely buckled into the Festiva, the cop car growing smaller behind me. The only answer I could come up with was an honest one: I don't know. I just remembered standing there and bringing the can to my lips—second nature, muscle memory, a little like breathing.

After a mile with no red and blue lights flashing behind me, I sped up, lifted the Coke can, and took another drink.

▲

JENNY'S STREET was empty and quiet. Like in her old neighborhood, the houses were so big I didn't understand what all the extra space was used for, the lawns green and trimmed tight, the sidewalks probably safer to eat off of than the plates of some restaurants I'd been to. I parked my car a few houses down and got out, Coke can in hand, the gun in the front pocket of my hoodie. With each step, I waited for every light in every house to flick on, people awakening, knowing there was an intruder in their neighborhood.

I crept around Jenny's house, the gate to the backyard was easily unlocked just by reaching over the fence and unlatching it. As I tiptoed across the grass, I thought about alarm systems, motion-detector lights, an attack dog even. I walked in the dark, looking for blinking red lights and listening for the growls of a dog, until I was in front of the back door, unscathed.

The glass in the door window was not very thick. I elbowed it twice and it gave away, spraying onto the hardwood below. I reached my hand through the opening, turned the handle from inside, and walked in, sweeping aside pieces of glass with my shoe. I didn't want Jenny or Adam to cut themselves on our way out.

I half expected Jenny to come running once she heard the glass shatter, but the house was pitch-black and quiet. Unopened boxes piled high, only the couch that Adam and I had sat on unpacked. I tiptoed around the boxes and listened for any sign of movement. The kitchen dark, the fridge empty, nothing for her to re-sort. I found her shoes at the front door and held them for a second; I'd never seen her wear them. When she left me with Adam, she'd been wearing slippers, fuzzy green ones. All the other times I'd delivered her pizza, she'd been barefoot. These shoes were sporty, all black with neon laces. I pictured her running in them. Sweat gathering at the top of her head, sliding down her face, over the slope of her nose, the curves of her cheeks, the point of her chin, dripping, her skin glistening. She looked relaxed—her body working, her mind free and clear, able to let her thoughts run as she did. These were the shoes that she'd wear when we took our long walks together.

I put the shoes down. I moved up the staircase quickly, careful not to take too much time on each step to think. A few images slipped through—Billy waking up to an empty bed, deciding to finally open the shed to see what I was up to, finding only crushed beer cans and a foam football, running to Mom's room, the two of them hollering my name, searching every corner of the house for me, the way the asphalt in the Eddie's parking lot glittered in the sun after I hosed it down. At the top I thought about the guy that picked up our garbage every Thursday, how he always whistled when he got out of his dump truck, as he heaved and threw each bulging, stinking bag, the tune and force of his whistling never changing, only stopping when he got back into his truck and drove away to the next house. I could never place the song he was whistling and it drove me nuts.

The first room was a closet, the second a bathroom, the third room completely empty. At the next room, the door got stuck halfway. I squeezed my way in and stepped on a stuffed hippo I recognized as King Cotton Candy, Eric the moose beside him. Stuffed animals covered the floor, Adam lay asleep without a single one with him in his bed. I watched Adam sleep and wondered what the stuffed animals had done to make him throw them all onto the ground. I ran a hand through his hair and whispered to him to sleep well, deep, everything was about to change.

The only room left was the one at the end of the hall. I stood in front of it, took another drink from the Coke can, and, for the first time since I'd left Dad's shed, I felt hesitation.

I'd hopped into the Festiva and sped down the 5 North. There was a high that came with being on the open road, alone, seeing Los Angeles fade behind me, the twinkling city lights burning out slowly. I'd never been outside of the city limits. Dad and Mom had always talked about a vacation for the three of us, but it never happened, always an excuse available—money, time, they could never agree on where they wanted to go, Dad liked cities and Mom liked nature. When I passed Glendale, I'd officially been farther from my home than I'd ever been in my life. All I could really think about on the way to Bakersfield was how good it felt to have the wind hit my face—I didn't think at all about what I would say to Jenny when I finally reached her.

I wrapped my hand around the doorknob. You don't have to say anything, I told myself. You just have to open the door and she will feel your shadow cross over her body and she will sit up straight in bed, having been awake for hours waiting for something without even realizing it was you, and she will know, even in the dark, even if she can't fully see the expression on your face, why you're here, that she doesn't have to say anything either, just has to get up and take your hand—I took another drink and pushed open the door.

The room was too quiet and I pulled the gun from my pocket. It didn't feel heavy, but sticky. Whether it was from my sweat or the gun's, the longer I held it, the more it seemed to melt into me. I saw an outline of the bed, but not much else. I took one step closer, two. No sounds or movement from the bed. My grip on the gun tightened and I worried that Jenny wasn't there, that she'd had an idea similar to mine and had hopped in her car, taken off down the highway before this new house became familiar and she found herself becoming as much a part of it as the plaster on the walls. I heard a cough and my heartbeat quickened.

I walked closer to the bed, and as I did, my eyes adjusted to the dark and I was able to make out a large shape hidden under blankets. I walked even closer and realized the large shape was not just one body, but two.

Jenny and Jim wrapped closely together. His arms around her midsection, his chin digging into her shoulder. Her head turned away from him and toward the window, a sliver of moonlight cutting her face in half. She looked pained to have him touching her like that, her body as far on the edge as she could go without falling off. Sleeping on the edge of the bed was no way to live. She should've been in the center of it with her arms and legs splayed out, the end of each limb touching a different corner and marking them sacred like pennies in a fountain, lipstick on a bare napkin, flags on mountains and moons and other places worth claiming, the spit of little kids on random sections of the sidewalk and street, a physical marker of joy so great it brimmed out of them in all forms and fluids.

Jim made a gurgling sound in his throat. I stared at him, not just a still, no-teeth smiling image, but a real and solid and fleshy presence. I raised the gun and pointed it at him.

My grip on the gun changed from stickiness to slipperiness. My hand started to shake and I had to bring my other hand to steady it. I kept the gun aimed directly at his forehead and I wondered how loud the shot would be, how it would echo throughout the house, how scared Adam would be, and what Jenny's face would look like when she woke up. His pillow was a light purple or blue and I tried to picture how blood and brains would look like against it. My finger was lightly squeezing the trigger when Jenny turned over and snuggled into the crook of Jim's neck.

I WATCHED THEM LYING TOGETHER, their bodies pressed close, drawn together even in their sleep. Her leg hooked around his waist, her arm draped over his shoulder; he pulled her tighter, and when they both sighed, deeply, I could see they were in love. Her breath must have felt so warm against his neck.

Jim suddenly looked handsome to me and, more than

that, I could imagine the comfort of his large body. She didn't move to Bakersfield because of him—she moved for him. She moved because when he left for work she immediately felt like the whole house got smaller. She paced room to room, touching each section of the wall, each grain of the carpet, trying to remember what he said the last time he stood there and there and there. Her heart must have bloomed to life every time she heard the door click open. She must have glowed when he kissed her cheek even when she was dying for his lips. During our kiss, I had no doubt that, with each passing second, she was comparing mine to his, how wrong mine must've felt—Jenny, I swear I didn't know, Jenny, why didn't you tell me? The strip of moonlight widened, and I noticed then that the shirt Jim was wearing was the one I plucked from her laundry basket the night I watched Adam, the one with tiny tooth holes in the collar, the one I put in my mouth and sucked on—his, not hers—she loved him and he loved her and I was a lonely, drunk pregnant girl in a home I didn't belong in.

I lowered the gun, drained the rest of the Coke can, and walked away. Before I closed the door behind me, I took one last look at them. They hadn't moved.

JENNY AND JIM didn't have whiskey, but downstairs they had bubble-wrapped bottles of wine in a box on the kitchen table.

I unwrapped one that had a label with French words and a black horse. The horse's mane was beautiful and long and flowing in a wind I couldn't see. The mane reminded me of Jenny's old ponytail and I pulled open each drawer, searching for a corkscrew, couldn't find one. I broke the neck of the bottle against the counter, poured some into the Coke can, didn't bother cleaning up the glass this time.

On the couch, I drank their wine and let my head fall back. I looked up at the ceiling and I couldn't project my future against it. I pictured so many things, but this was impossible. I stared hard, actually tried to see myself in a year, a month, a week, a day from where I was sitting. All I could see was pizza, booze, Los Angeles, and the inside of the Festiva.

I had a random memory of a day from a year or so back when I was alone at home. I had ditched school and was hoping that there was still some roast beef Mom had made the night before in the Tupperware in the fridge. I told the school nurse that I had a headache, a really bad headache, and I could barely see her face or the mustard stain on her cardigan. It was around 11:00 a.m. when I got back to the house, and I knew this because I had faked a headache to ditch third-period pre-calc to avoid a test—unit circles made no sense, and my graphing calculator was big and had buttons with squiggles on them that actually made my head hurt.

When I opened the door, I saw Mom sitting on the couch, Tupperware in her lap, roast beef in her hands, grease on her chin. Dad opened the door and walked in less than a minute after me, and then we all stood staring at each other. We all had places we should've been—Mom opened at Kmart on Tuesdays, Dad had just started a new job cleaning the bathrooms and mopping floors at a law firm downtown, Mrs. Keery was probably glaring at my empty desk. We knew this and we didn't say anything, just started laughing. We laughed past the appropriate amount of time, only stopped when our sides and lungs threatened to burst. We sat on the couch, not saying anything to each other, passing the roast beef back and forth, and watching a TV show that I don't remember a single part of. I sat in between them, their shoulders both touching mine.

I put my hands to my eyes and realized I was still holding the gun. The gun in my hand no longer felt sticky, or slippery, or much like anything at all. I pointed it at myself, looked down the barrel of it, and I couldn't see my future there either. I pointed the gun to the ceiling and, just to see, just to hear what it would sound like, I pulled the trigger.

Nothing happened.

I looked at the gun, opened the cylinder, and saw that there were no bullets in it.

I laughed and laughed and I don't remember much after that. I'm pretty sure I dropped the bottle of wine, which I only know from later, from looking at my hoodie and seeing little burgundy splotches against the gray fabric. The last thing I remember is distantly feeling hands grabbing my shoulders, my whole body being shaken. Through a tiny slit of light, I saw Jenny's face close to mine, could see she was yelling, but couldn't hear what she was saying. She really was beautiful, even with short hair.

EPILOGUE

I WAS FIRED FROM EDDIE'S.

I wasn't fired because of the incident at Jenny's. I didn't even think Peter, or Darryl, or Willie, or anyone at work found out about that. I just failed to show up for my shift and didn't call anyone back. Apparently, Peter and Darryl both called me several times. I tried to explain to Peter that the cell phone he'd been trying to call me on no longer worked, had broken a couple weeks back, that even if it had been working, I was in a Bakersfield hospital that day, wouldn't have been able to answer. He didn't care, told me that he could find plenty of people that didn't disappear and wind up in weird hospitals, people who had working cell phones.

I woke up the morning after that night at Jenny's without realizing how long I had been asleep or that I had even woken up. It just felt like I had closed my eyes, taken a very long blink, and when I opened them, I was staring out a window that faced a brick wall. I heard a whimper and I looked to my other side and saw an IV in my arm, Billy and Mom rising from chairs.

Billy told me in a monotone, looking not at me, but out the window at that brick wall, how he was woken in the night by a phone call and was half asleep when he realized what a strange woman was yelling into his ear. He and Mom were soon driving without even changing out of their pajamas.

"That woman almost called the police, you know. Her husband really wanted to, was horrified that a drunk, pregnant girl he'd never seen before had brought a gun into his home—his home, where his son slept—that this girl was clearly dangerous." Billy choked on the word "dangerous"; I looked over his shoulder to see Mom crying silently into her hands. "You're lucky the gun wasn't loaded and the woman insisted that you weren't dangerous, that you were just a girl who was in a bad situation, that you were having a hard time. But who is this woman and how the fuck does she know about your situation or the time you're having?"

Billy finally looked at me, no tears in his eyes. "Who is this woman?"

The doctor came in soon after and told me, in front of Billy and Mom, that I'd had a blood-alcohol content of .17 and that, given my state—he gestured awkwardly to my belly—this was highly dangerous. "You are pregnant," he said. "Heavy drinking while pregnant can result in miscarriage or stillbirth, and there are a range of lifelong physical, behavioral, and intellectual disabilities your daughter could be born with."

"My what?" I asked.

"What?" The doctor frowned. He was young, his hair blond and long, and his name tag didn't read anything funny, just said "Dr. Carroll." If this man was named Dr. Oldman, it wouldn't have been funny. I wanted to ask him if he was a surfer.

"You said my"—I tried to swallow and it hurt, the inside of my mouth tasted awful and stale—"daughter. You said 'daughter.'"

"Yes," the doctor said. "You are going to be having a baby girl."

I sobbed into my hands until maybe Mom, maybe Billy, maybe Dr. Carroll or a random nurse pulled my face from my hands and pushed me into their chest to stifle my sounds.

A week later, I got a new job, bagging groceries at the local supermarket.

Every hour I thought about quitting, but I was eighteen, didn't know how to do much of anything, twenty-one weeks pregnant.

It really wasn't that bad. The work was easy. Even a chimpanzee that had been hit over the head multiple times with a rock by his chimpanzee friends could've figured out a way to grab what was given to him, put it in a brown, recyclable bag, smile, and say, "Have a nice day."

The only bad moments were if people purchased a jar of pickles. When the jars were passed my way to be bagged, I just looked up at the fluorescent lights and hummed quietly. It must not have been that quietly, though, because on my third day Marina, the cashier I was paired with, leaned over to the cashier on twelve, jerked her head at me, and said, "Did Donnie give me one of those Special Ed high schoolers again?"

One day, Rita came into my lane. She didn't seem to be hurt in any way, but she never had seemed that way even when she was being hurt. We made eye contact when I passed her three bags and she said, "Thank you," and I said, "Have a nice day."

Another day, Darryl and a short guy with a mustache and a thick, neck-swallowing chin showed up in my line. I figured the guy was Carl after I watched the way he put his hand on Darryl's shoulder and told him to put the magazine back, there was no need to waste money on things like that. When I handed them their bags, Carl said, "Thank you," and I ignored him, looked at Darryl. He gave me a "Hey," nothing more. I gave him a "Hey" back. "Do you guys know each other?" Carl asked. I wanted to turn to him and say, "Yes, we do. And I know you too. I hope you realize how fucking lucky you are," but I just said, "We used to work together." Darryl took a bag of cantaloupes and cucumbers from me and said, "Thank you." I watched them walk out of the automatic doors, hand in hand, and said, "Have a nice day." Marina leaned over to twelve again and whispered loudly, "Donnie needs to stop hiring retards."

After my shifts, I didn't drive anywhere except home. Jenny's old street would've been on my way, but I took a different route. It added an extra five minutes.

At home, if Mom was there, I would sit next to her on the couch and watch whatever was on. We watched a lot of game shows, *Wheel of Fortune* mostly. As the pinwheel spun around, I would try to work up the courage to ask her all the things I wanted to know—was she able to look at me without thinking of Dad, did she like Billy more than she liked me, was she still excited about the baby, her grand-daughter, did she know I didn't hate her and never hated her, I worried she hated me?

One night, we were watching *Full House* instead of *Wheel of Fortune*, and I heard myself saying, "I just worry that I'm a lot like Dad."

Without turning from the screen, she said, "You are."

Before I could really process this, let it take me to a dark space, she continued, "You're smart and have an eye for detail. Your dad was always pointing out things he noticed, things I never would've seen myself. Your sense of humor is similar too, not a loud ha-ha, in-your-face kind of funny, but quiet, a little dark, honest funny, is what I always thought. It's why people liked him so much. Did you know that everyone in the neighborhood loved him? He had a way with people, connected to them in just one interaction, and it's because he never pretended to be any-one but himself. You loved tangerines growing up, could eat them all day. Your dad made sure to become friends with Steve, the guy who sells fruit by the freeway, so he could get them at a discount and you'd never have to ask if we had any left." The credits of *Full House* started to roll. Neither of us made any move to change the channel. "You have his eyes. On first glance, brown, but if you looked close, you could see how complex they were—light brown rimmed by a dark green, makes me think of moss growing on tree bark."

"I meant the bad stuff."

That kept her quiet for a moment. The credits finished rolling and a commercial about tampons began, women of all ethnicities running through a pure-green field. "He had his problems," she said, "there's no denying that. But none of that is your fault and nothing is decided. It's up to you to be more than him."

"I hated how he treated you, how he stole so much of your life."

A show I didn't know came on. It seemed to be about a group of dogs that were tired of their humans controlling their life. We watched the intro and then she said, "This is not where I saw myself when I first immigrated to America."

"What, like, Los Angeles? This house? This couch? Did you want one of those couches that massage you?"

She didn't laugh. "I don't even remember anymore what I imagined on that plane ride from Seoul to Chicago, but I didn't imagine this."

"I'm sorry."

She turned away from the TV then, looked at me, didn't say anything until I looked at her. "Don't be," she said. "I have more than I ever thought I would have."

BILLY HADN'T SAID A WORD to me since we left the hospital. The only time we'd really talked since Bakersfield was the first night back in our room. He'd asked me if I even wanted the baby, if I even loved him, and I'd asked him to stop yelling at me, I couldn't think when he was yelling at me.

I never asked what happened with the gun. I imagined Jenny holding it, being as fascinated as I was by its stickiness, holding it for a moment and wanting to fire it before tossing it in the trash.

Billy never brought up the gun either, but he came home one day with a large backpack full of textbooks and dropped it on the kitchen table, made Mom and me look up away from the TV. He spoke only to Mom and told her that he had just enrolled in night classes at the local community college and was hoping that, after a year, he could transfer to USC or a college like it, a college that could help him get a good job, a job that actually paid well and would allow him to provide for her and the baby. "I can't keep doing what I'm doing and stay sane." He didn't mention my name.

We were back to avoiding each other in the mornings. I finally got a new phone and sometimes he would call me or text me things he wanted me to grab from the grocery store—peanut butter, black beans, pizza bagels, whatever he needed to make dinner—but mostly my phone didn't ring throughout the day. I imagined him mowing lawns and digging holes, stabbing his shovel sharply into the ground and picturing my face where the point of the shovel hit.

He'd come home and shower before he went to his classes, and I'd watch him get dressed and look in the mirror, smooth out his button-down, flatten the cowlick at the back of his head, and nod approvingly before leaving the house again, not looking at me. It hurt just watching him walk out like I wasn't even there, but when I watched him watch himself in the mirror, he looked more like the boy I'd known in high school than he had in a long time—it made me warm thinking about him sitting in a classroom, diligently taking notes.

At night, I'd stay up until he got back from the community college. I'd get into bed on my side and he'd climb in on his side and we'd fall asleep, our backs to each other. But in the mornings, I'd wake up and my face would be against his chest, our bodies wrapped together. When I woke up, I'd quickly close my eyes again, slow my breathing, pretend I was still asleep—I could feel him do the same thing.

We would only move and fake-yawn once our alarm rang. Every evening, one of us would set our alarm a couple minutes later, neither bringing up why we were doing so.

JENNY SHOWED UP at the grocery store on a Wednesday three weeks after Bakersfield.

I had finished my shift for the night, told Marina we would hang tomorrow—we were friends then, had discovered we both loved watching NBA games, no matter what team was playing—and was about to get in my car when I heard a voice from behind me.

"Hey, Pizza Girl."

▼

I'D AVOIDED thinking about Jenny. I'd stared mindlessly at fluorescent lights for hours, been taking a different route home from work, I'd shouted at Mom a week ago when she suggested we order pizza for dinner, but as Jenny stood in front of me in that grocery store parking lot, I realized how avoidance was the most attention you could give something.

I fiddled with my car keys. She passed her grocery bag back and forth from one hand to the other.

"Why are you grocery shopping here?"

"I'm not. I called Eddie's first." she said. "I asked for you, but the guy working there said you were gone, got a new job. I had to threaten to talk to his manager for him to tell me where your new job was."

"Why do you have a grocery bag, then?"

"I was just hoping to run into you. I bought chicken nuggets and a jug of milk."

"The dino-shaped ones?"

"No, just the regular."

A woman walked up and unlocked the car between us. She only had two bags, but it seemed to take her forever to load them into her trunk. Jenny and I both watched her, and I'm sure she was as grateful as I was for a moment to collect ourselves.

The woman finally got the bags into her trunk, hopped into her car, and pulled away. I turned to Jenny and really looked at her then, straight in her eyes. "Do you even know my name?"

She looked blankly at me.

"You've never called me by my real name."

"I know your name."

"What is it, then?"

I'd never thought about our age gap until that moment, or maybe I'd never thought about it because I'd never wanted to think about it, had ignored the way she had always looked at me, like I was something semi-recognizable, a small flicker of something she remembered, but had mostly forgotten about, shoved to a dark corner of her memory. "Your name is Jane," she said.

More fiddling with keys, more bag passing between hands. "I'm pregnant too," she said.

"Oh." I looked at her belly, no bump visible yet. "Congratulations."

"Thanks. Maybe I'll name it Jane if it's a girl."

"My baby is going to be a girl too. Maybe I'll name it Jenny."

"That would be weird."

"So would your daughter being named Jane."

We both laughed. "Don't worry," she said. "We're probably naming it after Jim's mother, Margaret."

"I don't know what my daughter is going to be named yet."

In a lot of ways, it felt like we were talking how we'd always talked, as if no time had passed, as if I hadn't shown up drunk at her place and passed out on her couch with a gun in my hand.

She said, "I have the best story about my new neighbor and her pet iguana," at the same time as I said, "Why are you here?"

I could tell by the way her shoulders drooped that she had been hoping we'd talk and joke for a few more minutes before she'd say goodbye, take care, like she always did. I half expected her to pull out her wallet and fold twenties into my palm.

"I don't know," she said. "I've just been feeling guilty, like it was my fault that you were in that position."

I almost told her that, yes, it was absolutely her fault I was in that position. That if she'd never called in to Eddie's, never left me alone with Adam, if she'd never kissed me back, if she hadn't made me feel special, like the things I did and said mattered, I would've been okay. But I knew that was a lie and that, even if I'd never picked up the phone and heard her voice on the other end, I would've found something else to lose myself in—if you were pushed off a cliff, you'd grab hold of anything resembling safety.

"You don't owe me anything," I said. "It's okay, really. Just tell me about your neighbor and the iguana."

There was still more I wanted to ask her. What exactly I meant to her, how much of herself did she actually reveal to me, did she still miss me sometimes like I missed her—a missing that had no electricity, no lightning, or thunder, a missing like a hand digging into an empty chip bag searching for crumbs, any last salty bit, a missing more like mourning.

But we just talked about her life in Bakersfield—the classes she'd started taking at the local YMCA, how Adam wasn't playing baseball any longer, but was interested in painting now, spent hours in their backyard staring at blank canvases before he even reached for his paintbrush, and then he'd stare at the different-colored paints before he made another move, how Jim was coming home earlier than he ever had since they'd been married, he didn't even wear a tie to work anymore—and the more she talked, the more the desire to ask faded. Her hair had grown a little longer. It didn't flow freely and lightly down her back like her ponytail did, but it went a couple inches past her chin, and she seemed to stand straighter and looser at the same time, nothing weighing her down. She would never be anything more to me than what she was now. If we saw each other again, it would be by chance, or, if you believed in this kind of a thing, by the large invisible hands that were responsible for pushing and pulling people together.

Billy called me and I answered on the first ring. "Hi."

"Hey, if you're still at work, can you get some ground turkey and tater tots? Brussels sprouts too if they're on sale."

I looked at Jenny. She smiled back. "No," I said. "I've already left. How about I pick something up tonight and we eat with Mom. I saw a new Chinese-Italian-French fusion place opened up near us, and I don't know what that means, but I'm interested."

He didn't say anything for a moment and I was worried he'd hung up, but then he said, "Yeah, okay. Sounds good."

I hung up and put my phone back in my pocket. "I've got to go."

"Me too," Jenny said. "Take care, Jane."

I'D MOSTLY STOPPED DRINKING.

The second night back from the hospital, I'd been

unable to sleep and got up from bed, sure Billy was awake, and gone to Dad's shed. I pulled all the unopened beers I had from the mini-fridge and opened them, dumped their contents onto the backyard lawn. The next day, I bought a new lock to put on Dad's shed and drove to a freeway overpass, threw the key to the lock over it.

That would've been nice if that was the last time I ever had a drink. That was the shit that people said in AA meetings, the stories re-created in commercials that encouraged people to live better lives. Not even a week after that, I left the grocery store and parked out in front of a liquor store, begged seven different men and women before a homeless guy in a wheelchair agreed to buy me a six-pack if I rolled him to the McDonald's across the street and bought him two Big Macs and a large fries. I asked him if he wanted a soda with it and he shook his head, said he heard if you left a tooth in a glass of Coke for twenty-four hours it would dissolve.

I broke the lock off of Dad's shed that night with a pair of pliers and drank four of those cans, dumped the last two. The next week, the same guy bought me another six-pack and I drank three and dumped the remaining three.

In the twenty-fifth week of my pregnancy, I finished my shift and drove to the liquor store. I could see the homeless guy wheeling around the front of the store, but that time I didn't get out of my car. I pulled out of the lot and kept driving.

I drove past my street and turned around, almost turned onto Jenny's old street. I didn't know where I was going. My daughter had been kicking almost every day. It was mostly just a small kick or two here and there, randomly—when I was brushing my teeth, opening the fridge, locking my car, saying hey to Marina. But that night, as I pulled up to the liquor store, she kicked four times, in quick succession.

I kept driving, and my left hand drifted from the wheel to the top of my belly. My belly had grown significantly, protruding far enough that I'd had to move my driver's seat back a couple notches. My hand felt comfortable on the crest of it, and as I cruised down the road, no turns being taken, I started talking to my daughter.

"Her name was Jenny Hauser and every Wednesday I put pickles on her pizza."

Acknowledgments

While this book is fiction, my dad did tell me once that he thought everyone would be happier if he lived alone on an island and even just writing that out now, my heart broke a little. Nobody should be an island and I am blessed every day that I'm not, that I have so many people who helped me become who I am.

This list will be long and it could be even longer. I could probably make a whole novel of just thank-yous.

Thank you to Cara Reilly, Emily Mahon, Sarah Englemann, Terry Zaroff-Evans, Todd Doughty, Tricia Cave, Jillian Briglia, and everyone at Doubleday. Thank you especially to my editor, Lee Boudreaux. You not only helped me shape this book, but you ate messy chicken wings with me and asked all the right questions, cared about the answers, brought light and enthusiasm even when I didn't have it. None of this would be possible without you—let's split a bottle of Havana soon.

Much love to Tallboy, an artist that if you don't know, you

should. I've been a fan ever since I bought a shirt of yours at Roberta's. Honored to be the first book cover you designed.

Thank you to my agent, Eric Simonoff. You said my query letter was the worst one you've ever read and I'm just grateful you looked past that and still read my book, believed in it. Thank you also to Taylor Rondestvedt, Laura Bonner, Fiona Baird, and all the other believers at WME.

Thank-yous to my professors at Columbia University who gave me a space to grow. Special thank-yous to Elissa Schappell, Sam Lipsyte, Ben Metcalf, James Canon, Binnie Kirhsenbaum, Rivka Galchen, Lara Vapnyar, Anelise Chen, Matt Gallagher, and Darcey Steinke.

To my professors at USC, the people who helped me fall back in love with writing: T. C. Boyle, Marianne Wiggins, Dana Johnson, Molly Bendall, Susan Segal, Chris Freeman, and David St. John.

I believe friendships are the purest relationships in your life, the ones where nothing is asked of you but yourself, and I am so lucky I have so many. There are people I love that are sure to be left off this list (I'm sorry).

Cheers to my Scum Mansion boiz and gurlz: Youssef Biaz, Emily Rawl, Jackson Burgess, David Fulmer, Marta Olson, Skyler Garn, Katie Barreira, Austin Shaw, Nate Fulmer, Austin Smith, Mike Harper, and Jessie Land—you guys made college a beautiful, gorgeous mess.

Another glass raised to my Columbia Writing peeps: Evan Gorzeman and The Mango Deck, Anya Lewis-Meeks, CJ Leede, Kyle Kouri, Brady and Natalie Jackson, Mina Seckin, Michael Hanna, Nifath Chowdhury, SJ Collins, Nick Smatt, Christina Schmidt, Chris Molnar, Etan Nechin, Mina Hamedi,

Naomi Falk, Nathan Fetherolf, Claire Carusillo, Jarrod Harrison, Santo Randazzo, Bryan Perley, Isabelle Burden—can't wait to buy your books off shelves.

Molly Leonard, Cat Barnes, Lucy Sheinbaum, Sami Pastron, Ethan Fuirst, Hailey Noonan, Carlos Rivera, Brenna Gildenberg, Mark Sullivan, Alex Bailey, Lauren Tierney, Dylan Silverstein, Bobby Fitzpatrick, Jake Roberts, Josh Brandis, Alana Duthie—I will always be AVAIL for you all.

To my high school friends who ruin my life every damn time—Mayuri Patel, Nisha Puri, Lauren Gutierrez, Isabel Lee—fuck you all, love you all.

My oldest friends in the world, who knew me when I had a bowl cut and still talked to me. Albert Lim and Carter Beck—the youngest I've ever felt was drinking beers in the trunks of our first cars, talking about shit that used to mean something.

To the sports teams I've played on, to the wonderful teammates I've had and wouldn't have known if not for sweaty practices and rough games—PVPHS Panthers (shoutout to the basement crew), USC Women's Club Basketball, USC Hellions (Five Lokos), Columbia Pandemic.

Big, big thank you to my family. On both sides, I have aunts, uncles, and cousins who drive me crazy and love me hard and I hope I drive them crazy back, that they know that I love them even harder.

Thank you and I love yous even bigger than that are reserved for my brother Ryan, someone I wish I could be as brilliant and hilarious as, whose couch I still plan to live on one day. My dad—I'm sorry things haven't always been good between us, but I'm thankful a lot has been good with us and we still have time to fix the bad. To my mom, whose first name is my middle name—thank you for showing me how important words are, showing me their beauty and their fragility, how you can have all the pretty words and it means nothing if you can't perform the actions that back them up—you are my hero, a badass woman who made me believe from a young age in the power of women, whose name I'm honored to carry and have printed on the spine of this book.

ONE PLACE. MANY STORIES

Bold, innovative and
empowering publishing.

FOLLOW US ON:

@HQStories